UTOPIA 2000

UTOPIA 2000

Elizabeth Greenwood

The Book Guild Ltd
Sussex, England

The Book Guild Ltd
25 High Street,
Lewes, Sussex

First published 1994
© Elizabeth Greenwood 1994
Set in Baskerville
Typesetting by Book Setters International Ltd
Salisbury Wiltshire
Printed in Great Britain by
Antony Rowe Ltd
Chippenham, Wiltshire.

A catalogue record for this book is
available from the British Library

ISBN 086332 934 9

CONTENTS

'Have you come to a mere dictatorship, which some persons in the nineteenth century used to prophesy as the ultimate outcome of democracy?'

William Morris – *News from Nowhere*

PROLOGUE

The car slid out of Horse Guards Parade amid silence, carrying its passenger with the anonymity that was pursued by all since the end of the uprising. There were few people about; here and there small groups of sightseers provided touches of colour to the greyness of the November morning, but they showed little interest as the car cruised past.

'Why the black Rover?' asked Rebecca. 'My old Scout car would have done as well.'

The driver shook his head. 'Too battle-scarred. You know what the policy is now: we've got to play down the martial air.'

'You don't seem too put out by it,' she remarked dispiritedly.

The driver gave her a quizzical look in the rear mirror. 'These were my orders – to use the Rover. I'm not doing anything different now than I was before, when things were hot – obeying orders. Besides, we were all warned about the aftermath, the withdrawal symptoms, the dreadful anticlimax. You, of all people . . . .'

'Slow down, will you,' Rebecca said, anxious to cut short the driver's dramatic enunciation in which she detected an overtone of sarcasm, not at all to her liking.

They were driving past St James's Park. There, plainly visible from the road, was the little bridge where she and Oliver had stood so many times during their secret meetings before the start of the Rebellion. The sight of it shattered her, physically and mentally, and her reaction, so swift and unexpected, made her curse her own frailty. After all St James's Park was only a stone's-throw from Whitehall and she could not honestly say that up to now the proximity of the bridge had bothered her one way or another; she must have gone past it a hundred times in the course of duty without registering any particular kind of emotion. Fickle, she thought, she could never trust herself again. Within a few seconds the bridge had crystallised an experience, become a symbol. Memory's treacherous flood had risen up, leashing together a hundred fragments that had lain dormant. She saw herself standing on that bridge with Oliver while crowds of Londoners went about their business, mindless of them both and of their joint revolutionary schemes. On it they had opened their hearts and minds to each other, expressed their distaste of the present and defined their hopes for the future. On that bridge they had discovered they held many beliefs in common in spite of the difference in their temperaments: he was the visionary, the leader, and she, the follower, the disciple who listened spellbound as he unfolded his plans for radical reform. He was such fun to be with, she found herself thinking suddenly out of context. Whenever she felt discouraged, he would pick someone out of the crowds in St James's Park and mimic with such accuracy that she had to laugh. His impersonation was funny yet tender; she felt gentleness and kindness in his insight, as though nothing his intellect told him could ever interfere with the great love he felt for his fellow creatures. As a woman she had always regarded that kind of humorous exercise on the part of the male as a distractive device, a kind of smoke-screen to conceal the real issue, in other words to shift the relation on a sexless plane and she had considered the men who resorted to it as men of doubtful virility.

'You'll be late for your appointment at Broadcasting House,' a voice trailed through her reminiscences, 'if I

8

don't press on now.'

'Very well, then, press on,' she replied wearily.

The acceleration over, the driver cast another one of his quizzical looks into the rear mirror.

'Why the uniform, Captain?' he asked.

'What did you think I was going to wear?' Rebecca asked. 'A little black dress to go with the car? I never wear black, I hate black. Besides, isn't that what they would expect me to wear?'

'I guess you're right. The media are still the media even now, after the Purge.'

'You sound disenchanted.'

The driver gave Rebecca another glance in the rear mirror.

'You could say that, I suppose. It's just that I expected something different from you, that's all. Wearing that uniform you could arouse adulation, hero-worship. . . even start something. You know what crowds are like . . . .'

Rebecca smiled. What a captious fellow!

'For some of us,' she replied quietly, 'the Revolution was not fought in vain. If we did not conquer the masses, at least we conquered ourselves. I'll be guarded.'

The driver kept quiet for a while and then, breaking the silence again, said 'We went to Venice for our holiday this year. We always used to go to Venice, my mother, my brother and I before the trouble started.'

'Why Venice, always Venice?'

The driver chuckled.

'My mother likes it! Especially the music festivals.'

Oh, no, thought Rebecca, not one of those who live under a matriarchal system!

'It makes me shudder,' she said aloud.

'What does?' asked the driver.

'Venice,' replied Rebecca, 'there's something sinister about it. All those black gondolas with their mournful

9

shapes gliding like coffins. They destroy the liveliness and gaiety of the water.'

*   *   *

Rebecca sat down in front of the microphone. This then was the moment she had waited for with trepidation – the beginning of her last mission. At one point she had entertained the hope that Oliver, wherever he was, would be listening. That hope had been short-lived. The preparation of the broadcast, which was to be delivered in several parts, cleared her mind of sentimental haze; as she progressed with it, so she was able to adopt a more realistic stance. By and by she came to accept the notion that her speeches over the air, rather than forge one last spiritual link with Oliver, would in effect mark her entry into final autonomy. When the starting light went up, she began reading from her notes, feeling very calm.

'It is with a melancholy heart and a certain sense of loneliness that I sit here to record some of the events which led up to the Revolution. Many of you over the past few weeks have requested that I should describe what it was like to be a Freedom Fighter in a Mission Unit during those momentous times. In complying with your wishes, I hope to achieve two things – firstly to make clear to you what a long way our country came up from apathy and dereliction; how much dead wood was hacked out by common intent to free the roots once peace was won, and, secondly, by so doing to find relief from the emptiness left in our lives by the departure of our beloved leader, Oliver Carrington, who simply vanished from our midst a few weeks ago . . . .'

*   *   *

'What are you watching, Edwin?' his mother shouted from the kitchen.

10

'What do you think? Our Rebecca, of course!'

'Oh, her! *La Fille du Régiment.*'

The driver chuckled. His mother was a witty woman; her quips descended in judgment on all things, whether physical or spiritual, shrouding them under a mantle of prosaic apparentness, which was a manner of reducing them all to an equal degree of triteness against which there was no appeal, no matter how lofty they might have been in the first place. This he found amusing, even outrageously funny, especially when her peculiar sense of humour was aimed at people or things that transcended the ordinary, as was the case with Rebecca or old paintings in Venetian churches. If Rebecca was foolish enough to appear on a television screen in that silly uniform of hers, then his mother was justified in dealing with her in her own particular brand of levelling wit. At this juncture he could not help but remember the time when gazing up at a religious painting in a church in a small village on the outskirts of Venice, he heard his mother say, 'Look, Edwin! Never let your left hand know what your right hand is doing.' His mother was pointing at the figure of a female saint at the centre of the picture whose right hand was hitching up a voluminous white robe high above a shapely thigh, while her left hand clasped the scriptures to her bosom.

Edwin opened another can of beer and chuckling truculently looked up again at the television screen. Rebecca's voice was droning on, issuing from those thin lips of hers that the make-up artist had not succeeded in making appear any fuller. Her utterances, spoken in clipped strands, made her sound as distant, as unimpressible, as ever. Her elocution, which Edwin found particularly irritating, matched her long bony face with its pointed chin and slightly sunken cheeks. The furrows made her cheek-bones appear somewhat high and promi-

11

nent. The only softness round her face was provided by a mass of black, curly hair that fell lightly to her shoulders. He should have been howling with laughter – what '*fille du régiment*' ever looked like that? Normally they were buxom wenches. He just wasn't able to see the funny side of it, so upset was he by the tone of the broadcast.

'. . . When the seeds of the conflict that opposed us to our countrymen were sown, I was a very ordinary person,' Rebecca went on, 'I possessed no academic qualifications, only technical ones: I could handle a camera well. When it came to ways of life to choose from, in the social class into which I was born, my options were few; the contemplation of most of them left me disinterested. Politically all I knew was that certain things in our society made me happy and others made me unhappy, but I could not tell why. My misery when it afflicted me was dumb, shapeless, awkward to carry about and my happiness, when I was blessed with it, transcendental. Then one day, everything fell into place: my country needed me, and others like me, I joined the Revolution . . . .,

Just then the telephone bell rang and covered the sound of Rebecca's voice.

'I'll take it, mother!' Edwin shouted in the direction of the kitchen. His mother's hands were smothered in flour; she always baked on a Friday night to soothe her nerves, she said, before the weekend.

'Yes,' Edwin muttered into the receiver. 'Well, what do you expect? I imagine there's worse to come . . . . What can I do about it? . . . . Censorship? You're right! They won't do a damned thing, just let it ride for old times' sake, although it's contravening instructions . . . . Let me know if you hear anything . . . Of course! 'Bye!'

Edwin shrugged his shoulders as he put the receiver down. Censorship! Since freedom of speech had been abolished there was no need for censorship. Only accre-

12

dited people spoke and they weren't going to be suppressed by their own side. Rebecca was, after all, a heroine of the Revolution.

'Who was that, Edwin?' his mother called from the kitchen.

'Oh, just an old friend.'

'What did he want?'

Edwin turned up the volume on the television set and the room boomed with the maddening sound of Rebecca's voice. He snapped off the top of another beer can; he felt in a rabid mood.

'. . . Farm machinery such as hedge cutters, roadsweeping tractors and verge-mowing ones were confiscated; the lads who operated them were rounded up by soldiers and sent to Youth Camps for further education. Almost simultaneously all over the countryside there appeared gangs of handicapped people; they came out of mini-buses that had trailers in tow in which were kept gardening tools of every description: shears, forks, spades, mowing-machines, mini-tractors. Each gang was led and supervised by an Educator. Wherever one travelled in England, these people, who would normally have led useless lives, were busily engaged in hedge trimming, digging, mowing, sweeping, re-seeding and planting. Whole areas of decaying woodland that had been neglected by irresponsible landowners were cleared and restored to health by these handicapped people . . . . One day our Leader, Major Carrington, rode past one such gang of disabled conservationists and he stopped to speak to them. They crowded round his tank and cheered him and asked if they might be allowed to climb on his vehicle and ride with him a little way. Unfortunately a team of American journalists, who had been chasing our leader all day, finally caught up with him. Cameras clicked, flashed; our leader was furious. He snapped his fingers at his bodyguard. In a trice these heavily-armed men in camouflage suits had seized all the reporters' photographic equipment. This created an uproar and after representations were made through the proper channels, a press conference was called. Our leader came in person and spoke to the American journalists (as most of you probably know, he never used a spokesman): 'Gentlemen', he began, 'Mark Twain, one of your most celebrated authors, once said: "In our country we have three unspeakably precious things, freedom of speech, freedom of conscience and the prudence never to practise either of them." Gentlemen, I am a prudent man. Good-day to you,' and with these words he left the conference. People were amazed that he, a simple Army man, could command such sophisticated arguments with which to exculpate himself and his Regime. At the conference their cameras were returned to the American reporters but not the films . . . .'

Edwin gave the television set a mighty thump with his foot. An outrage – it was nothing short of an outrage. She had to deify him! Because he had escaped from her clutches, she had to turn him into an icon, he the most irreducible of men! She had to take away from him all his warm-blooded frailties and petrify him and, having petrified him, enshrine him, so she could have him all to herself to worship for ever and ever, and what was worse she had to seduce gullible people into following her to the Shrine. So much for her reassurance 'I'll be guarded' made to him in the car when he drove her to the studios. She was faithless; she'd say anything to have her own way. Her betrayal was all the more damnable for it.

Edwin buried his red, sweat-beaded face in his hands and cried.

PART I

1

On a clear day, a knoll crested by three pine trees, attractively positioned together, with the tallest most umbeliferous one rising above the other two, stood out against the sky with appealing beauty. Much further on, to the extreme right along the horizon, the eye was stopped from ranging any further by another clump of elegant pines marking a final boundary to the sandy ridge. Cattle grazed on the huge heather-tufted slopes that lay below the brow. Their figures, dotted here and there either singly or in groups, were dwarfed by the sheer size of the Down, the face of which was striped from top to bottom by wide gullies in varying shades of umber. These weals were in fact channels cut by the tracks of tanks as they clambered up and down the hillside, grinding their way through sand, loosening boulders and roots.

Standing in a low-lying field at the foot of the hill, Oliver kept looking up at that panoramic view; its majestic sweep elated him. Time and again he returned to the same spot at the base of a gully where he could stand and stare at the impressive Down, and, if he were, as was often the case, rewarded too by the sight of tanks out on exercise, then he was well-pleased. Since he had returned from West Germany, a redundant 'tankie', he missed the company of other tank men and practically everything else to do with tanks. Here, in this blessed spot, he loved to listen to the monotonous whirr of tanks tracking up and down those picturesque slopes, now loud, now faint, then finally fading away, when the exercise was over, to return the Down to its eerie silence through which the wind itself dared not whistle. Today, Oliver was in luck; the large red flags flying at regular intervals all along the top of the Down heralded military activity; they were flown when the Army intended to detonate explosives on the range. Oliver left the place where he had stood a long while to admire the scenery and started up one of the many sandy tracks that led to the summit. The path rose steadily through patches of heather. Being a tall, long-striding man he soon emerged on to higher ground where the gradient became steeper. Loose stones and clumps of turf rolled under his feet as he scrambled up the last few yards to the top. With pleasure he noted that he had retained enough fitness from his days on active service not to slide backwards through the scrub. There were as yet no signs of tanks. They must have been on the reverse face of the Down; he could hear far away the sound that gratified his ears, faintly animating the unseen side, investing it with a promise of benefaction, like a wave rolling onwards from the offing to the feet of the tyro who waited on the shore.

That Keeper's Down held a dual fascination for him, he understood perfectly well: up here, the thought of the sea was intimately linked with that of regimental life, on the same register of pleasant associations. All that sand, all that marine flora – the pine trees, the gorse bushes, the broom – the sea had left behind millions of years ago; the Down was, in effect, wherever he looked, a primeval barrier jutting out high above the tame greenery of the low-lying approaches where man had had his way in guiding the frond. He had grown up by the sea. From an early age the sea had drawn him into a secret relationship, unveiling for him her myriad faces, so he passed from one ecstasy to another. By accretion over the years, a store of blissful memories linked to the sea built up inside him in layers that reached so deeply in his affections that he need never know want. . ..

A man in uniform, a sergeant, stood before Oliver staring at him as though he had seen a ghost. At once Oliver realized reminiscing about the past had temporarily obliterated his knowledge of the here and now.

Smiling he said, 'You have before you a retired soldier, Sergeant, not a spook. I know they say the Down is haunted, but I can assure you I am not Dick Turpin. Oh, I know, the red flags. . . I shouldn't be here.'

'Falklands? Belize?,' the sergeant asked, looking nervously over his shoulder.

Oliver laughed.

'Nothing like that, I'm afraid. West Germany. Tank Regiment. Major Carrington, redundant. The truth is I can't keep away from tanks.'

'Don't tell me!' the sergeant replied, 'I've heard it all before. There's something about those damned machines that sends men crazy. Once a "tankie", always a "tankie".'

Oliver saw something moving in the bushes behind the sergeant's shoulders.

'Are those your chaps in camouflage suits? It looks as though they're breaking from cover.'

The sergeant pivoted on the spot. 'Get down, you pimple-riddled pixies,' he shouted, motioning his men down with his hands, 'what do you think this is? Babes in the Woods? Any minute now the RE will start blasting!'

'I wonder what they saw. . .,' muttered Oliver.

'People say there's a puma roaming the moor, but, knowing my men, it's more likely to have been a bit of skirt.'

The sound of galloping hooves coming from the left

made both men look in that direction. A girl on horseback was approaching fast on the top track where the flags were flying.

'Congratulations, Sergeant,' said Oliver, 'you know your men well, but you'll have to take back the bit about the skirt – the lady's wearing breeches.'

As the rider drew level with them at an alarming speed, the first explosion went off. The noise reverberated through the air with prodigious force, making the horse rear. Oliver saw the girl falling backwards; he sprang forward, followed by the sergeant. The girl had not relaxed her grip on the reins; when they reached her she was being dragged round and round, while the animal kicked up clouds of dust, prancing and snorting, as upset by the sight of its rider on the ground as it had been by the blast.

The sergeant bent down over the girl while Oliver took hold of the horse and pacified it. The girl slowly let go of the reins. She lay motionless on her side, keeping her eyes shut, her face smudged with sand.

'Whatever made you do a thing like that, miss?' the sergeant asked, 'there's red flags flying all over the place, warning civilians to keep off the range.'

Oliver tied the horse to a nearby tree then, drawing the girl gently up by the shoulders, he made her sit up straight so he could examine her head. As far as he could see, apart from a few minor cuts and grazes, she had not suffered any injury to the skull.

'Come on,' said Oliver, 'let's stand you up to see if you have broken any bones.'

With the sergeant's help he got the girl up on to her feet. She stood still for a minute then, brushing the sand off her eyes, she began stooping this way and that as though she were about to lose her balance.

'My hat! Where's my hat? I was wearing a hat.'

'I'm glad to see you're not suffering from amnesia,' Oliver said jokingly.

The sergeant, for fear he should be asked to search for the hat, shuffled up to Oliver's side.

'Sir' (it was the first time he had used that form of address and he did so in a whisper), 'I've got to get back to the men. God knows what they're up to, ruddy peeping Toms,' and looking sideways at the girl he muttered, 'Whatever possessed her? It does not make sense. . .. Well, goodbye, Sir. See you some other time perhaps?'

'Oh, definitely,' replied Oliver, 'once a tankie, always a tankie. Isn't that so, Sergeant?'

'Wilkes, Sir. That's what they say, Sir.'

Turning to go, the sergeant stopped by the girl; she had found her hat and was brushing it with a paper handkerchief.

'You should wear a crash helmet, Miss'. With these ominous words, he started across the heather in the direction of the recruits he had left behind. Oliver watched him go, stumbling against clumps of roots as he strode on faster and faster, until he disappeared over the top. A second explosion shook the almost empyrean silence of the Down, followed by a third and a fourth in quick succession, making the horse tug at the reins as it ran backwards after each report. Quickly Oliver untied it and, stroking its neck, led it over to the girl. As he covered the ground that separated them, he kept watching her. He found her behaviour puzzling in the extreme. What exactly was he looking for? Signs of fear? Nervousness? Gratefulness? Pain? Relief? She evinced none of these.

'You know, what the sergeant said is true: you should wear a crash helmet.'

This last remark provoked no reaction, either in favour or against.

'Mind you,' Oliver went on, 'my father, who was a tank

Commander, always rode into battle hatless, standing up in the hatch. He used to say wearing a helmet was the surest way of having one's head blown off.'

She took the horse from him without saying a word; it was plain she was not going to let him humour her.

'Are you sure you're all right?' Oliver asked, feeling more and more flummoxed.

'I'm fine, really. Thank you.'

It came as a tremendous relief to him to hear she still possessed a voice.

'Sometimes, people suffer from shock moments after an accident. Shock has a kind of delayed action. . ..'

'Honestly, I'm fine. I'm used to falling. I know how to fall.'

'All the same, I think you should have a skull X-ray as soon as possible. Shall I help you back on the horse?'

'No, I'll lead him; he has broken into a lather.'

'Is it far?'

'Where?'

'Where you have to take him.'

'No, not very far.'

After she had gone, he realized he did not know her name. He ran after her and soon caught up.

'I haven't introduced myself. Oliver Carrington, ex-British Army on the Rhine.'

She stopped walking and turned round to look at him.

'Stella Simmons.'

He had the distinct feeling she resented having been made to disclose her name; she sounded sullen. Before she turned away, he had time to notice there were freckles on her face: one of them had been bleeding. He also saw a torn hair-net hanging down the side of her neck. He stepped in front of her.

'Please, let me.'

Gently he pulled down the hair-net and handed it to

22

her. Holding his breath, he thought he'd dare; he'd tempt providence; he'd push his luck.

'Do you ride here often?' he asked.

'No. The going is too rough. The Army have ruined it with their tanks.'

He thought *Touché* and attempted a magnanimous smile.

'I'm staying with friends in Aldershot. I wondered. . .. Well, I intend to visit the Army range often. . .. Maybe I'll see you again, on horseback possibly?'

He read anger in the look she gave him before turning away, but that might have been a projection of his own sense of guilt at having pressed himself on her when she was still shaken. He watched her go as far as he could see down the long, straight, sandy track where she had first erupted into his and Sergeant Wilkes' ken; then the gradient of the moor took her from his sight. Intermittently he caught glimpses of her and the horse between gaps in the thickets that lined the downhill path, and then she was gone. Inexplicably, at that point, he felt depressed. He began walking about aimlessly; while he ambled he kept turning over in his mind the exchanges they had just had, meagre and unsatisfactory as they were. As the sergeant so aptly put it, it didn't make sense, none of it. The girl must have known the firing range well; she must have been familiar with the routine of the red flags; the horse was kept nearby, she herself said so. He began to suspect she had been upset to start with; too upset, having got on the horse, to remember to look out for the danger signals on the moor. The way she was pushing the horse, it looked as though she were running away from something frightening enough to suppress her instinct of self-preservation. This would explain why she seemed almost disappointed at having been rescued and offered no thanks to her rescuers. But all this was pure conjecture on his part. He shrugged his shoulders; he really had no lead. There was no point in hanging about; the sergeant and his men were nowhere to be seen; the blasting had ceased, as well as all sound of tanks in action.

Gradually, as he started walking downhill to get back to his car, the beauty of the landscape obliterated all other thoughts; his spirits began to lift. A pleasant south-easterly breeze enlivened the atmosphere. The air was clear, so clear, that Oliver could see every detail of the scenery which lay at his feet. He stopped walking and stood still for a while. This was a place, he felt, where men might be tempted to err on the side of idealism, conceive great thoughts, dream of worthwhile deeds. That Nature in its unpremeditated state should have such an inspiring effect on someone such as himself, he thought amazing, for he was essentially a practical man. The Army had satisfied his yearning for discipline and a sense of purpose; it had bound his aspirations within strict limits. His father had been a regular soldier; there seemed to be no reason for not following in his footsteps. As a boy, however, he remembered he had wished for some endeavour that would employ him outside the realm of selfish material-istic pursuits, one which would eventually give him, and possibly other men, a new identity different from his father's, more corporate, less formal perhaps? He was not a religious man. Even up here the contemplation of this heavenly view did not conjure up the idea of divine worship. Spiritual regeneration to him was just another embarrassingly individualistic attempt, in which one could easily become bogged. Formal Church rites, he considered, were necessary to satisfy the needs of those who derived comfort from them; he did not feel lowered by their observance, nor elevated by it. What he sought was something altogether different, for which the past offered no model.

2

Oliver stepped into Colonel Wallace's house full of misgivings. Hours before the appointed time for the cocktail party, he had turned over in his mind the same thoughts. Had it been a mistake to accept the Colonel's invitation? Was it right for him to go on mixing with Army people, brother officers still in uniform, still in military jobs? At times he felt like an outcast. On the other hand, by refusing the Colonel's invitation, he might hurt his feelings and the Colonel was an old friend of the family. Slowly he signed the visitors' book, as if to gain more time to stop wavering. From where he stood in the hall, the hum of a party in full swing reached him, deadened by a pair of stained glass doors. He hesitated before walking through as another thought struck him: what if Colonel Wallace had invited him because he felt sorry for him, because he imagined he was suffering from a severance syndrome? Of course, it was true; he was afflicted, but only with nostalgia for a way of life, the only one he had ever known. For years his job had been to bring the right team with the right equipment to the right place at the right time. Had he ever done anything else? And what prospects had he now in civilian life to practise logistics on a similar routine basis? The idea of a drink appealed to him; it would nip self-pity in the bud. Resolutely he started steering his tall, lanky figure through the party in

25

the direction of the bar. Several times, as he navigated, he thought he spotted Colonel Wallace's bald pate, but it kept disappearing behind other people's heads. During his progress he noticed several ex-soldiers from the Rhine and ducked to avoid indulging nostalgia about the good old days or giving vent to recriminations about the Government. The Government had very little to do with the soldiers' plight; the Government was only an instrument; the country was the trouble, the Body Politic. The country did not care.

'So glad you could make it, dear boy,' Colonel Wallace had crept up behind him, flanked by an orderly carrying a tray of drinks. 'What will you have? Sherry or medicine, as your father used to call it?' asked the Colonel.

'Medicine, please.'

'Is that what you need then?' Colonel Wallace asked, giving Oliver a searching look.

'Of course not!' exclaimed Oliver.

'You had me worried for a minute. Hardly the sort of thing I'd expect from you.'

Oliver felt relieved; the Colonel had not asked him to his party out of pity.

'You mustn't let things get you down,' the Colonel went on, helping himself to a drink from the tray. 'I know it's pretty hard to take. First West Germany, then Hong Kong.'

Oliver looked down.

'It's a mess, Sir, a real mess. What are we going to do with all these people?'

'I tell you what: I'll introduce you to a pretty girl,' the Colonel said, laughing, 'there's no better tonic than the conversation of a pretty woman. We're fortunate in having quite a few here tonight. How about General Flemington's daughter?'

'Which one is that?' asked Oliver.

'Tall, dark girl over there.'

'Yes, all right.'

'Follow me.'

They edged their way through the guests, taking care not to spill their drinks.

'Rebecca, I'd like you to meet Oliver Carrington, recently returned from the Rhine.'

'Infantry?' she asked abruptly looking Oliver straight in the eyes.

'No, Tank Regiment,' replied Oliver.

'Oh,' she said 'will you excuse me, Wallace. I promised an old friend of Father's I'd have a drink with her before she left and it's getting late.'

Both men watched her make her way through the crowd to the other side of the room.

'Strange girl,' muttered Colonel Wallace. 'I knew her father well. He was in the Infantry.'

'You're using the past tense,' Oliver remarked.

'Yes, he died in a helicopter accident outside Hanover; she never got over it. There was some talk of foul play. You know how Intelligence like to make out that they infiltrate everywhere. Personally I thought it highly unlikely. I had known Flemmie all his life . . . . Rebecca's mother couldn't stand Army life; she left when the child was three, eloped with some Consular officer. I don't think Rebecca has seen her mother since.'

'Is she . . . unattached?' asked Oliver stealing glances at the girl across the room.

'As far as I know, but she doesn't tell me everything!'

At that moment Colonel Wallace noticed a guest he had not seen before.

'Ah, Stephen, you old gaffer! Will you excuse me, dear boy.' Patting Oliver on the back, the Colonel walked away.

Oliver decided he would make his way across the room to where General Flemington's daughter was standing.

27

There was some urgency in doing this in case she decided to leave with her father's friend, but as he pushed hurriedly through the guests, he saw her coming back into the throng; instead of catching up, he collided with her.

The twinkle of amusement in her eyes, as he bumped into her, did not escape him; her eyes – large, black, lustrous – were the most striking part of her face.

'Major Carrington! Tell me, I've always wanted to know. What did it feel like to be protected by a carapace?'

'I take it you are referring to my tank?' Oliver asked trying to emulate her flippant mood.

'Yes, of course!'

'Running the risk of being fried alive is not my idea of a sheltered life. Still, I suppose, if you compare our lot with that of the Infantry, we don't get bitten by mosquitoes quite as much as they do.'

She glared at him, and he felt mean at having mentioned the Infantry, remembering what Colonel Wallace had said about her father.

'It's not easy, though,' she went on, looking at him with searching eyes, 'to dismiss the thought that perhaps deep down tank men are guided by a desire to return to the womb, to be insulated from the rest of the world.'

'I hope my mother's womb was never as noisy or smelly as a tank, but, I'll grant you this, yes, tank commanders do enjoy the corporate feeling their tank gives them, when the hatches are down and they share its private world with the crew. It is a unique experience.'

'Ah,' sighed Rebecca, 'the bond of man with man! Hunting in packs or playing games, or scrambling on to suburban trains leaving their womenfolk behind! It hasn't changed much since the Cave Age, has it?'

'You don't seem to me to be the type to be left behind in a suburban house,' Oliver remarked quietly.

'You mean I wouldn't put myself in that position?'

28

'Can you tell me how we got into this kind of conversation in the first place?' Oliver asked.

She burst out laughing and extended her hand to him.

'Let's shake hands and drink on it, like old troopers. I'm a photographer; I've been all over the world, you know.'

'Really?' said Oliver, taking a couple of glasses from the orderly who was passing by.

'Yes, I wanted to study history, but my father thought his many postings abroad would enable me to travel, to get a different kind of education.'

'And did it?'

'As a photographer? Oh yes. I shot history in the making. Pretty gruesome at times.'

The crowd around them in the room was beginning to thin. From a distance they saw Colonel Wallace amble towards them between small groups of people.

'Well?' he asked jovially, 'you two busy exchanging memories of the Rhine?'

Oliver shook his head.

'Being nostalgic about the good old days is not going to solve the problems of homelessness and unemployment that vex my men.'

'I know,' said Colonel Wallace, 'skilled in the use of lethal weapons isn't a qualification for civilian employment. The lucky ones are the Electricians of the Royal Engineers and the HGV drivers in the Royal Transport Corps, not to mention the electronics and computer experts. Unlike your chaps, they're finding jobs in Civvy Street.'

'Is there nothing we can do to help these men?' asked Rebecca with a frown of concern.

'The trouble, my dear,' replied Colonel Wallace, 'is they're not a force; politically, they're disenfranchised. Nobody gives a damn about them. By nobody, I mean no politician gives a damn about them'

'But this is terrible!'

'I wouldn't worry your pretty head about it,' Colonel Wallace went on, 'we can't set the world to rights, can we? Go on taking your beautiful photographs. By the way, I thought your last exhibition at the Photographers' Gallery was first-class. I found the aerial photographs fascinating, couldn't take my eyes off them.'

'I've got a good pilot,' Rebecca said smiling.

'You'll have to excuse me both. I think some of my guests are leaving.'

'You take aerial photographs as well?,' Oliver asked after Colonel Wallace had left them. 'That's interesting. I was looking for someone who would photograph a tract of Army land for me from the air. Could you . . . would you accept the commission?'

'Major Carrington, I can see you are not the sort of man to take no for an answer. If this tract of Army land you mention is reasonably near Blackbushe Airport, then yes, I'll do it for you. You'll let me have a map of the area, won't you?, care of Colonel Wallace. And now you must excuse me. I feel tired.'

At once he sensed he had upset her, why he did not know. She, so natural, so extrovert, suddenly appeared inhibited; she lost the directness of manner which constituted the main part of her charm. A shadow had fallen between them.

Oliver thanked Colonel Wallace for his cordial reception and promised he would try and accept what the Colonel called 'the fortune of war', corrected by him as the 'misfortune of war'.

'We had it good for so long; now comes the last post metaphorically speaking, and we have to call it a day. It's as simple as that, dear boy'.

Much as he liked Colonel Wallace, Oliver could not

30

help thinking the Colonel's words had a stale ring to them; as commonplaces they failed to make an impression. How could they carry any weight placed against the long tales of woe he heard at his friends' from ex-tankmen? Almost every day he had to cope with a stream of distressed callers, to the extent that the repetitive occurrence at the house became an embarrassment to him.

'Don't be too sympathetic, Oliver,' the Colonel warned on parting, 'if your chaps feel you're a willing listener, they'll take advantage. Human nature, dear boy. Let the proper authorities deal with them. After all, that's their job.'

While returning to his friends, on foot, Oliver thought how right he'd been not to drive to Colonel Wallace's party. He needed time to regain self-control. He was troubled by many conflicting thoughts; many contradictory feelings unsettled him. Not the least of these was the sense of disloyalty Colonel Wallace's attitude to the redundancy problem instilled in him; he could not condone its rigidity. Then he was puzzled by his own request to General Flemington's daughter that she took aerial photographs of the Army range; it had been so spontaneous! What on earth had possessed him to make such a strange request? Was it prompted by his desire to have a memento of the place where he had met Stella Simmons or was it a stratagem to keep in touch with Rebecca Flemington? For years he had functioned within an uncomplicated system with hardly any questions asked, thanks to a kind of nonchalance which struck him in retrospect as having verged on lunacy. Now he was searching for answers to questions he had to formulate himself. In connection with this process he considered it perfectly rational that he should interrogate himself; what he found odd was the necessity to examine the existence of others, in particular the lives of two women, fortuitously implicated. In the case of Stella Simmons, for instance, he was not sure whether his interpretation of her frailty was based on facts or a figment of his imagination, which flattered his male ego by making out that he had rescued a damsel in distress, he for whom the Army had no further use. When he went over the circumstances of her riding accident, a number of points indicated that she would have coped on her own, had he and the sergeant not butted in. As for Rebecca Flemington, the element of provocation he detected in her social conduct might have been subjective. The way in which she, and probably other professional women, behaved normally in Society, he would not have been familiar with, having spent the best part of his life in the company of men in a closed military world. As a soldier he believed aggression invited and justified attack; in finding Rebecca Flemington aggressive, when perhaps due to her background, job etc., she was merely evincing signs of self-assurance, did not this so-called aggressiveness he thought she displayed serve as a jolly good excuse for considering her fair game? No longer at a loose end, in her case, he would play the part of conquering hero. He was flabbergasted. As a practical man, there was only one course open to him to put a stop to this unhealthy introspection – action. He would go back to the Army range, to the spot on the Down where he had seen Stella Simmons disappear, follow the path (Stella Simmons had said she did not have far to go) to try and trace her. As for Rebecca Flemington, he would not play a waiting game; he would send her an ordnance map right away.

3

If there was one thing Oliver could not stand, it was to see Army wives crying. He had just watched about thirty of them weeping, inside a courtroom, the wives of ex-servicemen who had served under him in West Germany. It was a piteous sight. Unable to bear it, he had left the courtroom before the end of the session. Serious issues had been raised in his mind by the business dealt with by the Court. Anger, indignation, even revulsion for the Army that had nurtured him, continued to disquiet him outside the courtroom. These were extreme reactions in a man who had always thought of himself as being of a placid disposition and as such they were not welcome. What he had seen and heard inside the courtroom had shaken his conscience to uncharted levels as well as upset him viscerally, an unusual combination of effects, which his behaviour reflected. He kept pacing up and down the pavement and as he paced, so he kept looking around him, casting anxious glances. Was this England? He could hardly believe it. To put an end to his confusion, he felt tempted to approach passers-by and ask them point blank, 'Am I standing on English soil? Is this really England? Please tell me truthfully,' but at the last minute he refrained. The people he had gone up to looked at him out of puzzled eyes before going on their way. He realized they would not have understood if he had accosted them.

They looked well-fed, well-dressed, in reasonably good health. What concern of theirs was it that, after years of service, men in their prime with young families to raise were legally evicted from Army quarters that had been home to them? For an eviction order to be served on them, they were classified as Irregular Occupants. Overnight they became Irregular Occupants of the quarters the Army had housed them in when they were recalled from garrisons overseas.

What concern of theirs was it, Oliver asked himself, as the pedestrians drifted past him outside the Court, that those same men had no civilian prospects? The conversion training offered by the Ministry of Defence was just not long enough or thorough enough to equip them with civilian qualifications of any bargaining worth. Without civilian jobs they were unable to support themselves and their families, let alone buy houses in the South of England. What nation humiliated its soldiers thus and, worse, got the law to do the dirty work? The men inside the courtroom were decent chaps. Oliver knew some of them well. They were not very bright perhaps but all of them understood, when they signed up, that at any time in the course of duty the country could require of them that they lay down their lives. True, the fear of unemployment had driven a lot of them into the Army and Necessity had relegated the thought of Death in Action to the remotest region of their consciousness; nevertheless the thought of Death was one they had to reckon with sooner or later. They were committed . . . .

The men were beginning to file out of the courtroom. Oliver searched among them for a tall sergeant who had been in his regiment. Directly he saw him he went up to him and shook his hand warmly.

'Thank you, Sir, for coming,' said the sergeant, 'it was a great help to know you were there. The wife's grateful too;

only she's too upset to speak; she can't stop crying. It's the thought of losing the children that's killing her.'

'What do you mean "losing the children"?' asked Oliver. 'When did this come up?'

'Well, Sir, that's what the Army welfare officer told us, prior to the hearing. Now we've been evicted, if we don't accept the Council's offer of a flat in a high-rise estate, our children, all four of them, could be taken from us, put into care, you know . . . .'

Sergeant Bates stopped to put his arm round his wife's shoulders and then went on. 'You see, Sir, officially we're squatters in our own homes and children aren't allowed to squat. That's the long and short of it.'

'After fifteen years of service!' exclaimed Oliver.

'Yes, Sir, fifteen years of service and what do I get at the end of it all? A court judgment against me and blackmail over the children.'

'One good thing is with fifteen years' service you are eligible for severance pay,' said Oliver attempting to sound jolly.

'That's right, Sir! Four thousand pounds! Just enough to build a potting shed. They're treating us like dirt.'

'What Albert says is true, Sir. They've made me feel like filth. I'm sure a lot of the other chaps here present feel the same,' echoed another serviceman in the group.

Encouraged by his mate's candour, a corporal came forward to speak to Oliver.

'I served in the Gulf, Sir, and I did a turn of duty in Northern Ireland and still they're evicting me and my family from our home.'

'Where is your home, Corporal?' asked Oliver.

'On the Goose Green estate, Sir.'

'Where's that?' asked Oliver.

'In Farnborough, Sir. Do you know what the housing officer said to me, Sir? He said, "Why don't you go back where you came from". Well, I come from up North, Sir, Newcastle to be precise, and what would I be doing up there after twelve years in the Army? My wife was born in Farnborough; her folks live there. Farnborough, Aldershot, Rushmoor, that's where we've always been with the Army, round that area. What can I do? Advertise? "Hero from the Gulf seeks well-paid job with family house Farnborough area"? I can imagine the response.'

'I don't know,' mused Sergeant Bates. 'There's always the Drug Barons, the Arms Dealers, the white slave traffic. You could be an asset to them!'

'Thanks very much!' replied Corporal Nash. 'The wife would love that! No, I went in when I was sixteen and I can't imagine myself doing anything else.'

Oliver was not deceived by the men's banter; their jocular mood camouflaged a deep-seated anxiety. Their well-ordered way of life, based on clean living standards, had collapsed. They were not unscrupulous enough, or cunning enough, to find another founded on compromise; some people just did not possess a talent for conscience-bashing.

'They've put every kind of pressure on us that they could, Sir,' Sergeant Bates went on. 'As Irregular Occupants we had to pay double the standard military rent. Where did they think we were going to find the money with no earning power? As I said, it was blackmail, pure and simple. Either we outstayed our welcome in Army quarters, and our arrears of rent ran into thousands of pounds which we couldn't pay, or we moved into a highrise council flat, the only one offered to us, and put our children at risk.'

'What do you mean? I don't think I've got this right. I thought you said your children would be taken away if you did not move into a high-rise flat?'

'I think you should go and take a look at the estate

where the flat is, Sir, then you'll know what I mean. There are about thirty ex-Army families already housed on the estate; they all say it's the worst place they've ever lived in. They've nicknamed it Hitler's Bunker. Kids throw eggs at their windows.'

'Friend of mine got his new motorbike stolen the first week he was there,' said Corporal Nash. 'He'd bought it with his severance money to scoot around for jobs.'

'Please, Sir,' pleaded Sergeant Bates's wife, dabbing her eyes with her husband's handkerchief, 'Come out and have a look for yourself. You have to see it to believe it. We were plain-living folks in the Army. We're not used to that sort of set-up.'

'If you decide to go, Sir, if I may be allowed to make a suggestion,' said Sergeant Bates, 'go there after dark, after 11 p.m., then you'll know why we would be putting our children at risk by accepting the Council's offer of a flat on the Copeland estate.'

Oliver searched their plain honest faces. What, he wondered, had prompted Sergeant Bates's plea for a night-time visit? He remembered Colonel Wallace's words of advice. 'Don't be too sympathetic or they'll take advantage.' He could hardly pay heed to those words now. He felt involved for better or for worse. Army wives were drying their tears; he could not let them down. The men's recourse had been to him; he could not remain aloof. His sense of commitment sprang not so much from the distressing tales of bullying he had just heard as from the emergence of the spectre of influences hurtful to children.

'Look,' said Oliver, 'I don't think we can stay here any longer, right on the Court doorstep. They'll have us for unlawful gathering or loitering if we don't move off! Sergeant Bates, you come to the house tonight. We'll make arrangements then for my visit to the Copeland

Estate.'

'You'll go and take a look then, Sir?' asked Sergeant Bates, tremulously, hardly daring to believe what the Major was saying.

'Yes, I'll go, but only if you pledge yourselves not to breathe a word about it to anyone. None of the military men on the Estate must know of my coming.'

'Yes, Sir, I give you my word. I'll not tell anyone,' replied Sergeant Bates solemnly.

'Right,' said Oliver, 'we'll disperse then. *Auf Wiedersehen.*'

4

'If you're telephoning about the aerial photographs,' Rebecca said as soon as she recognized Oliver's voice, 'they're not quite dry yet.'

'No, I'm not; actually yes. Do any of them show a horse in a field?' asked Oliver.

'I thought your regiment had converted to tanks, Major Carrington.'

'Indeed, years ago, but the memory of those far-off Cavalry days lingers on and not only the memory but the idiom as well.'

'Really?'

'Yes, for instance, for climbing in and out of tanks, we use the expressions "mounting" and "dismounting". But that's not what I am telephoning about. As you may remember, when we were at Colonel Wallace's party you asked was there anything you could do to help my men get over their resettlement problems?'

'Yes . . . .'

'Well, there is. You could do something to help them.'

'But that's ridiculous! What could I do that would be of any use? My father was an Infantry man, anyway.'

'You could take more photographs.'

'And how would that help, I ask you?'

'It's really too complicated to explain over the telephone. Briefly, your photographs would be used to foment public opinion.'

'Thank you very much!'

'Taking them would involve some risk. You'd be working in the dark, at dead of night, secretly.'

'Planning a Commando raid, Major Carrington? hope you've laid up a good store of burnt cork and coal-dust.'

He thought he'd ignore the irony; he needed her skills.

'Well, no, not quite, more like a reconnaissance under cover of darkness.'

'It sounds exciting and where exactly is this little midnight excursion going to take place?'

Oliver hesitated, knowing he was laying himself open to more irony.

'In Farnborough.'

'In Farnborough! My, my! If you'd mentioned Salisbury Plain, I would have said you had daring, but Farnborough, that's really adventurous!'

'Actually, the operation requires quite a bit of nerve, or rather a strong stomach for squalor, so my men tell me, but that shouldn't be a problem, should it, judging by some of your past assignments?'

'Oh dear! The scenario's getting worse and worse,' Rebecca replied, laughing.

Oliver had not heard her laugh so light-heartedly before.

'I can't wait to hear the rest!'

'I'll send you a drawing of the exact location, with the time and place of *rendezvous*, that is if you are willing to come.'

'Of course, I'll come, if only for the thrill.'

'You do take photographs in the dark?'

'Of course! Who doesn't nowadays?'

'Right. See you on the day.'

Oliver hung up. The step he had just taken was an important one; yet it generated mixed feelings, not an overall one of satisfaction. This second commission closely following the first one was likely to be far more consequential. Alone he had decided to take up the cudgels on behalf of his men; by commissioning Rebecca he was involving her in a scheme he had much at heart. He was drawing her into an enterprise the outcome of which he could not foresee. During its course, which might turn out to be lengthy, the chances were he would resort to her photographic skills again. A fortuitous chain of events, by virtue of its inevitability, would bind her to him, turning her into an ally. The prospect worried him. He was not used to discussing his thoughts with subordinates. As an officer he had received and communicated orders. Few people had enjoyed his confidence. The intercourse he had with Nature as a boy had been too personal for him to share with anybody; moreover, it had been too sensuous to put into words. For that reason he had never felt the necessity to convert feeling into thought and thought into words .... Come to think of it, he knew very little about General Flemington's daughter. Already the fact that she was Army seemed to implicate her by right, without any valid reason: he who had always had tons of steel under him felt he stood on shaky ground.

Nor did he consider he stood in a more secure position in relation to Stella Simmons. His desire to start a relationship with her, if only out of curiosity, had found no ingress. He did not know when he would have the chance to look at the aerial photographs of the Army range to see if they at least could help to locate the horse. He had been unable to carry out his plan to go back to the spot where he had last seen Stella Simmons and explore the countryside around it; a constant stream of aggrieved servicemen had kept him confined to quarters. The thought occurred to him that by organising a visit to the ill-famed high-rise flats on the Copeland Estate he had in effect started to deal with the men's problems and could responsibly leave the house for one day. The weather was not very good; wind and drizzle combined to create the usual dismal Sunday weather. He would return to the moor to try and trace Stella Simmons, though due to the bad weather she would probably choose to stay indoors rather than go horse-riding. He, on the other hand, might not get another chance to go exploring.

5

Sunday was, of all the days in the week, the worst one. The weekly boarders had gone away for the weekend; the staff had retreated to their bungalows. After this routine exodus Darley Hall subsided once again into its old domestic dream; silence took it over and coaxed it. Now and then the staircases creaked; the furniture let out faint sighs, but apart from those occasional sounds, nothing stirred. For Stella, Sunday was the time of greatest helplessness. The house, rid of all pretence, was free to brood over the outrage that had been perpetrated against it during the week. Its Elizabethan past and all the layers of living that had filled it over generations rose in silent revolt against abuse; there was nothing Stella could do to protect herself from its mood. During the whole of the weekend, she felt possessed by nervousness and spent most of the time fruitlessly trying to calm down. Every moment of the day and night brought apprehension of hidden dangers. She had tried to deal with the tension by getting out of the house, but her last excursion on horseback during half-term had been a near disaster. She felt guilt and shame when she recollected what happened: guilt at having put a horse at risk; shame at having been found out. Those two men on the moor, the major and the sergeant, they sensed something was wrong, especially the major; he kept probing.

There were only two things she could do; one was pray, the other rush to her room on the top floor and look at the marvellous view of the garden from the window. She was not a religious person, but she found that saying formal prayers induced a kind of trance which banished fear. The view too had a therapeutic effect.

There was an additional anguish attached to Sunday round which the whole day seemed to gravitate. Time crept towards that particular Dominican ordeal with a ponderous regularity that Stella deemed diabolical; it was the five o'clock tea with the headmistress and her assistant, Mrs Cunningham. They had instituted this ritual out of compassion for Stella who had nowhere to go. Her mother was a widow; she had remarried and started another family late in life, in Guernsey. Stella was welcome there, but the seven hours' sailing that separated the island from the mainland made it impractical for her to pay short visits, and then her mother was always so busy, engaged in a series of last-chance pregnancies that made in-roads on her health, much to Stella's chagrin. Stella wished she could have confided in her mother, but the thought of aggravating her condition by unburdening herself on her stopped her from speaking out.

Today she could not pray. Looking out of the mansard window was the only option. She stole upstairs to her room, clambered up into the window seat. The view she gazed at struck her once again as being the most perfect Nature could design as landscape. Her eye also ranged over the field where her horse was grazing; he looked contented, flicking off the odd fly with his tail, starting up from time to time at the wind's bidding. Unable to suppress a cry, Stella withdrew suddenly from the window. She had caught sight of a man standing outside the wicket gate at the short side of the field. She felt sure she had seen him before – it was that Major Richardson,

44

no Carrington, the one who had come to her rescue on the Down. She ran down the stairs as fast as she could, thinking she would go round the back way to avoid being seen by him; she could not miss that teatime appointment. Half-way down the stairs, she halted her flight; it was silly to run away when only a few minutes earlier she had been deploring her lonely circumstances. Although it would take a lot of explaining, inviting Major Carrington to tea with the headmistress would make the Sunday ritual less of an ordeal, if he were willing to go. On the other hand, this impromptu invitation might make her appear eager or forward, which she was not.

As she emerged under the porch of Darley Hall, she decided to keep calm. Descending the front steps she looked over to the left, then to the right in the direction of the field where she kept her horse, then heading across the lawn towards the headmistress's bungalow, she acknowledged Major Carrington's presence by waving to him. It was the coolest thing she had done for a long time. With baited breath she walked on, wondering what response her sign was going to evoke. For a very long time her steps were the only ones crunching through the gravel on the drive. When she reached Miss Beaumont's threshold she turned round sharply. Major Carrington was nowhere to be seen; the vast expanse of lawn that separated the big house from the bungalow was empty. She rang the door bell and waited. Her nerve ends started to riot again. Giving Major Carrington a sign of recognition had been a mistake. She should have screamed and run. Not that screaming would have made any difference; Darley Hall, apart from its gut reaction to Philistine invasion, never showed any sign of interest in anything; it evinced total indifference. She had been sent there to acquire qualifications; until such time as she became a qualified librarian, she had no means of supporting herself

45

outside. Out of the wisdom of the very poor, that consideration aborted all thoughts of flight at any time.

The door opened and she walked in.

*   *   *

Before it became a tarred road, the track which wound down from the top of the Down rose up on to a hump bridge; by following it one was able to walk over the railway line that separated the heath in the hinterland from cultivated ground in the fore-side. That track was the one where Oliver had lost sight of Stella Simmons on the day she had her riding accident, he was quite sure of that, having followed it all the way down from the place at the top where she had started to lead her horse. Past the bridge, fields opened out on both sides into large vistas, hemmed in by chestnut woods. As one went on, the road became wider. Rusty barbed-wire fencing ran alongside it; here and there tree trunks had fallen across the wire and made it sag. Oliver felt sure that all the land that lay to his left belonged to one estate. Behind an avenue of chestnut trees he thought he saw a horse grazing in a field; this prompted him to take advantage of a gap in the barbed-wire fencing rather than go on wending his way round the outside of the property by following the road. An incredible amount of dead wood littered the way across the approaches, hampering his course. He also had to step over old enamel buckets full of holes, broken sheets of corrugated iron that reminded him of Nissen huts, dilapidated feed troughs and capsized water tanks inhabited by tadpoles and water boatmen. Having picked his way through carefully, Oliver reached the grass edge of a well made-up drive on which he noticed fresh tyre marks. From where he stood he could see on the right the entrance to the drive, flanked by two stone pillars with finials, and, on the left, several hundred yards further up,

46

an Elizabethan mansion with attractive chimney-stacks. In a field nearby, the horse he had glimpsed from a distance now appeared quite close. Oliver recognized it immediately; the animal Stella Simmons rode, he remembered, had four white socks, and these showed above the grass which in places had been close-cropped. This encouraged him to think he was not far from achieving his quest. He walked on towards the house, taking care to remain on the grass verge. As he drew level with the field where the horse was turned out, he saw a wicket gate by the side of the drive and stopped awhile to lean against it. He now stood in full view of the house. The drive opened out on to a very large lawn, then forked to either side of it, making access possible from two convergent directions. The Elizabethan frontage of the house bore the stamp of authenticity; its proportions were exquisite. Unfortunately, the overall impression was spoilt by later additions of less fortunate aspect; these made it virtually impossible to isolate the genuine nucleus and enjoy it on its own. While he stood gazing at the facade, a diminutive figure dressed in blue suddenly appeared under the porch of the house and started coming down the front steps. The wind and rain must have caught it by surprise; a hand flew to the coat collar and buttoned it up. Then the figure stopped and waved. Oliver was so astonished that he stood stock-still and during the few seconds he stared, the figure vanished down an alleyway into the thickly grown parts of the grounds. How long a time elapsed before he could shake himself up, he did not know. He sprinted in the direction of the alley, ran down between rows of rhododendrons and reached what looked like a bungalow in the murky light, just in time to see Stella Simmons disappear inside. Rain trickled down his face and neck; pelting down those paths lined with thick overhanging bushes had made him sweat too. He was conscious that both his appearance and the business he pursued were undignified, to say the least. He began to doubt his initiative and within a few seconds ended up regretting it. But having come this far, what alternative was there? Going back soaked to the skin and frustrated as well? He would persevere. A light went up in the bungalow. Taking care to approach on the side the rooms were in darkness, he crept up to the back door, then crouched below the level of the window sill so he could get round to the front, where Stella Simmons had entered the house. When he got almost round, he noticed a tall narrow window. He unbent slowly, just enough for his head to emerge above the sill and peeped. A light was shining through from a brightly-lit room beyond; thanks to its effulgence, he was able to establish that he had circled almost right round the house and was now standing outside the hall. It was a narrow ante-camera fitted with glass doors, more like a porch built-up as an afterthought to keep out the weather. On the wall opposite he noticed a tall, old-fashioned hat-and-coat stand complete with umbrella trays, mirror and glove drawer. A couple of jackets hung on it high up. On top of the glove drawer was a felt hat, a Homburg of average size; for a minute the base thought crossed his mind that Stella Simmons was visiting a lover and that her hand sign had been made in jest, to taunt him. A beam of light fell on the hat. It looked the colour of grey pearls. There was something objectionable about its silvery smooth appearance, a hint of Dandyism Oliver thought, but it might have been an effect artificially created by the translucency of the glass in the window, filtering the light that shone on the hat. Instantly, Oliver's determination to find out what Stella Simmons was up to stiffened. He hurried past the front door on bended knees, padded to a large window where most of the light emanated. Very slowly he began to straighten up his back

48

and, taking care to observe from an angle at which he could not be seen, he peered inside. Stella Simmons was sitting on the edge of a large upholstered armchair, holding a cup of tea. Although he could only see her obliquely, he was struck by the stiffness of her position. By contrast, the other two people in the room were sitting comfortably, looking perfectly relaxed. One was a middle-aged woman with an ample bosom and strong stout legs. Below a very large, very square chin, she wore pearls which made her neck appear very thick. The tea tray stood on a small table by her knees which were rotund and made her skirt ride up. The other person in the room was much older. She had white hair, cropped all round and was wearing a grey tweed suit; she sat facing Oliver. He noticed the shoes she wore were black brogues and her stockings were grey. Looking at her more attentively, the notion came to Oliver that she must be the owner of the Homburg he had seen in the hall on top of the glove drawer and that the colour it appeared to be was not an illusion – it matched the older woman's suit exactly. For a split second the discovery stunned him; then he recovered and quick as lightning bolted to the front door and rang the bell with all his might.

The middle-aged woman answered the door.

'Is Stella Simmons here?' he enquired. 'I was told she is looking for a companion for her horse. A friend of mine in the Household Cavalry has a horse he wants to retire in the country.'

'Stella . . . ?' the woman gasped. 'Oh, yes, of course, Stella Simmons!' and turning round towards the lighted room she called out, 'Stella, it's for you!'

He heard the sound of a tea cup being put down and waited, fearfully. He tried not to show any emotion when Stella Simmons appeared in the doorway, looking peaky. Deep down he felt an absolute brute.

'Miss Simmons. I'm Major Carrington, ex-British Army of the Rhine. I'd like to see the field where you keep your horse before it gets any darker. I understand you are looking for a companion for your horse. A friend of mine would have just the right animal for the job'.

He took the blue coat off the peg where it hung conspicuously on the stand and handed it to her, just to show he was not prepared to put up with any delaying tactics. Without saying a word, she took the coat from him and put it on, then she turned to the woman who was holding the door.

'Please apologise to Miss Beaumont. I had no idea my advertisement had been noticed.'

The woman simpered.

'It shall be done. Run along then, Stella.'

He side-stepped to let Stella go first then, doffing his hat to the woman, turned round and went out of the door.

Stella walked ahead in silence till they were out of sight. A little way down the rhododendron path she stopped and turned round to face him. Tears were streaming down her cheeks.

'Why did you do this?' she asked, looking up. 'What gave you the right to butt in? We are perfect strangers.'

He lost his temper with her.

'I should be the one asking questions!' he shouted. 'What is this place? Answer me! Here am I out for a pleasant Sunday stroll through a favourite beauty spot of mine and where do I end up? Answer me!'

'I don't know ... I don't understand what you're driving at ....'

'I'll tell you where I ended up! I ended up in a den of iniquity, that's what! And what I'd like to know is what were you doing in there? I thought you were the healthy outdoor type!'

She turned her back on him and resumed walking.

50

They had reached the top of the rhododendron path and had emerged on the forecourt of the big house.

'And what is that?' he shouted pointing at the Elizabethan building, 'tucked away, miles from anywhere? An ancient monument on the plain of Jordan?'

'I don't know what you mean,' she whined. 'The name of the house is Darley Hall.'

'An Annexe, I presume! Stella, you can't stay here!' He was amazed at the strength of his own feelings. Words rushed out of his mouth at an alarming rate. He did not know he cared that much, about Stella, about her circumstances. She was an innocent and he feared for her safety. He could not stop himself.

'Look at you! You're tense, you're worried. You nearly killed yourself that day on the moor. There is something wrong; I know there is; you must let me help you.'

He put his hand on her arm to stop her running away, but she managed to wrench herself from his grip and darted towards the house without saying goodbye. He listened for a minute to check if anyone had followed them from the bungalow, but there were no sounds of footsteps anywhere. He was alone. Cloud rack scudded overhead, ceiling the sky very low. The atmosphere oppressed him. The drizzle had turned into rain. He stood there getting drenched, listening to the sound of water dripping down from the trees on to his clothes. He felt 'beached' on the edge of darkness like an old tank hit in battle and abandoned to the vagaries of the tides on an alien shore.

6

They had left Sergeant Bates and Corporal Nash to stand guard at the bottom of the stairwell in one of the towers on the Copeland Estate, while together they began to investigate the floors one by one. From time to time, as they padded along the corridors, Rebecca Flemington set down her photographic equipment to fit new flash-bulbs to the camera while Oliver kept watch. Once or twice during the early moments of their nocturnal exploration they heard the hoot of an owl, the signal they had agreed on beforehand with the men in case of danger, and they took the wall. Secrecy was all-important. Army people were considered public enemies by the residents of the flats; if any of them were to be found snooping around at dead of night, trouble might break out and Oliver's plan be jeopardized. A lot of scuffing about was going on between floors; on one occasion they heard the sound of broken glass. Rebecca dreaded the thought of one of her cameras becoming damaged; it was an old Leika she was very fond of; with it she had successfully covered several ethnic wars.

'What's that awful smell?' whispered Rebecca, as she bent down to pick up one of her cases. 'It is quite nauseating.'

'Urine,' replied Oliver.

'How do you expect me to photograph that?'

'I don't know, look for a corner where they urinate, I suppose. It shouldn't be too difficult; the stench is terrible.'

'I thought all these blocks had mod cons. May I use a torch?'

'Yes, if you promise to be careful. Junkies favour corners. From what Sergeant Bates tells me, there are quite a few about after dark.'

He was able for a while to follow the glint of the equipment she carried, then gloom swallowed her as she penetrated the heart of darkness. Once or twice, while he waited for her to return, he thought he heard Sergeant Bates giving the alarm and he wondered if Rebecca had paid proper attention to it; some of her accounts of wartime coverage indicated that she could be quite reckless. With a sigh of relief he greeted her back out of the shadows.

'What happened? You were gone hours.'

She gave a short, muffled laugh.

'I lost my bearings in the dark!'

'Any luck?'

'Yes, I think so. I also found a lot of used syringes heaped in a corner.'

'Did you manage to photograph them?'

'Of course! All was quiet so I went ahead and did it! I even brought you back a couple!'

'Splendid! Now we must hurry back to the first floor, where we saw those Nazi slogans scrawled out on the walls. It is important that we get photographs of all the graffiti, obscene or otherwise, and that includes swastikas. I understand from Corporal Nash they're all over the walls. The place certainly deserves its nickname . . . .'

'What's that?'

'Hitler's Bunker, that's how the men call it.'

Rebecca Flemington took a step closer.

'Is that how you are going to foment public opinion?' she whispered. 'Ex-servicemen's families dumped by Council in National Front stronghold, I can just see the headlines. Oliver, are you sure you know what you are doing?'

'No, but I can try and find out by searching my heart,' Oliver replied with a smile. 'Technically, I suppose there'd be no reason why those photographs couldn't be blown into posters?'

'None at all, but the question is, would I be willing to do it?' She tossed back her head and gave a quiet giggle.

'Of course, you'll do it and you'll even photograph Army wives marching to Whitehall in their thousands, holding your posters as banners high above their heads.'

'I always thought you were a bully from the moment I met you. And what, may I ask, will our mutual friend Colonel Wallace think of all this?'

'You know what he will think. What do people his age think?'

*　　*　　*

Oliver was thankful that he had been too busy to have the time to brood over the stalemate he had reached with Stella Simmons. After the fiasco of that dismal Sunday afternoon sortie he had sent Stella a note care of Darley Hall, giving her his friends' address in Aldershot and offering his help, if ever she needed it. He had written 'help' but what he meant was 'protection'. There was no doubt in his mind that Stella needed protection. She was at risk. All he could do was hope she possessed an inner sense of propriety, a biologically sound, female instinct that would come into play at the right time and assist her.

Rebecca Flemington had produced some quite amazing prints of their midnight excursion into the maws of the Copeland Estate. There was more than a touch of poetry in her photographic work. Even the heaped syringes of drug addicts showed artistic flair in the sensitive way she had handled the angles at which they were shot; they reminded Oliver of razor shells, stacked up high on a beach. Against a background of drawn curtains, a window smeared with egg yolk, to which the remains of a shell still stuck, had a surreal quality which made a lasting impression. All these proofs of talent should not have surprised Oliver; Colonel Wallace had been unstinting in praising Rebecca's work. He seemed to regard her with admiration as well as affection and he was not the sort of man to squander compliments. What puzzled Oliver was Rebecca's upright aloofness; it seemed to contradict the warm, sensuous quality he detected in her work. The eye that selected the angles at which she shot objects was, after all, guided by taste; not only were the fruits of its discrimination original, they were also intense. Oddly, only the originality of her art transpired in the way she functioned as a social being – unbending, unyielding. Oliver could not imagine her leading another mode of life. Her autonomy seemed a form of immunity, which at times verged on impertinence – nobody should be that exempt from contingencies. The manner in which she tackled her job, the way she conducted her life, her choice of clothes (Oliver had never seen her in anything but Safari suits) appeared to be dictated by strong compulsions which emphatically proclaimed that there were no alternatives. To suggest any would have been tantamount to insulting her.

For a while Oliver's enthusiasm for the artistic merit of Rebecca Flemington's photographic work blurred the appalling squalor of the living standards on the Copeland Estate, as her camera had caught them. When the dazzling power of her talent decreased through familiarity and at last he was able to look at the prints soberly, the crudity of the environment they depicted stood out: the Copeland Estate was no fit place for ex-servicemen to raise their children; an alternative had to be found.

At that point Oliver felt he had become becalmed on the turgid waters of practical life. Unable to move in any direction, he took this opportunity to look back over his shoulders at his past life. What he saw caused him no small measure of consternation. More constructively, however, he understood, that this backward glance had in fact become possible through detachment from his old self and the knowledge afforded him some comfort. He was actually able to define the state he had been living in all those years as limboesque, a kind of fool's paradise away from the main stream of life where men had to fight to obtain what they wanted, not merely rely on promotion. This gave him the motive he needed to spring back into action. He took to roaming through Aldershot. During his long solitary walks he often gazed up at dilapidated Army properties; in some streets he saw entire rows of them. It was difficult to understand why, with so many men to resettle, they remained vacant. Gradually, while perambulating, Oliver elaborated a scheme whereby Army families would be able to buy those old properties through a building society, renovate them and eventually live in them. To test the validity of the scheme, he had first to sound the men of his regiment; they were less likely to be diffident. Their response was unanimously favourable and, on the strength of it, Oliver extended the proposal to men in other regiments. They expressed a similar interest. Before long Oliver had the support of thousands of ex-servicemen. The next step was to start a campaign. Associations which represented the soldiers lobbied MPs. Army wives went to Whitehall to hand in a petition proposing a deal for the purchase of one particular row of houses. Building societies were approached regarding the funding of renovation. Then the scheme foundered. What galled Oliver was the fact that the people who scuttled it were the very authorities in charge of resettlement. The Ministry of Defence sold the dilapidated row of houses the families had in mind to a property developer for less money than the soldiers offered. 'Nobody wants us, Sir,' was Sergeant Bates' resigned comment when Oliver broke the news to him of the Ministry's decision.

Oliver felt the blow keenly. The men had been humiliated; they had been made to feel that they were nobodies. In addition, Colonel Wallace chose not to conceal his relief when the scheme miscarried. He had expressed doubt on the affair throughout and had openly criticised Oliver's 'meddlesome conduct'. The temptation to give a post-mortem was just too great when the axe fell.

'I told you so, my boy. One thing I am sure of, the Ministry didn't mean their action as a snub. The fact that you are taking it as such vicariously for the men only serves to show to what an extent you have gone off the rails. You gave the problems of those pigheaded bigots an importance they just do not possess in the eyes of the Ministry, or in anybody else's for that matter. You must put an end to all this tomfoolery before things go too far.'

To unsettle Oliver further, an embarrassing incident occurred involving one of the men in his regiment, a lance-corporal with two children. Fed up with being an Irregular Occupant and owing the Ministry arrears of rent to the tune of two thousand pounds, the man jumped the guns and moved into one of the old Army properties selected for renovation while the campaign for possession was still in progress. He was immediately ordered to clear out.

'That's all right, Sir,' commented Corporal Nash out of his own brand of wisdom, 'he'll end up in Hitler's Bunker; the Council will see to that; only his prospects there will be worse than anybody else's 'cos he's an Asian.'

Oliver thought that on the whole the men had behaved well; they had taken the blow with dignity. Whenever he had moments of doubt or discouragement, their attitude of fatalistic forbearance, enlivened now and again by the sarcastic remarks of the more articulate amongst them, acted as a spur. Willy-nilly he had become their champion. Neither indifference nor bullying tactics had succeeded in altering their vision of what decent living quarters for themselves and their children should be like; that soundness was well worth fighting for. The Retreat had sounded. Strategy suggested that, when it sounded for the first time, it was time to redeploy. But first he had to ask the men if they were willing to extend their mandate until such time as he succeeded in bringing this crucial issue of living standards to a satisfactory conclusion. He felt that he had stumbled into leadership more by accident than judgment. Events had caught him at a loose end and he had slipped into a situation where his position had never been defined. How could it have been since he, an officer, was dealing directly with troopers, with underdogs? He had taken advantage of a *status quo*. In actual fact, he had no authority, no power, except what was vested in him by the men when they let him act on their behalf. Now he wanted more than just the tacit acceptance of a conventional relationship. He wanted a covenant with the men – to be admitted by mutual consent as their head.

Oliver knew that he could trust Sergeant Bates and, to a lesser extent, Corporal Nash. He took both men in his confidence and asked them to organize a meeting with all the military families that had been re-housed on the Copeland Estate, as well as all the Irregular Occupants who had outstayed their welcome in Army quarters around the Aldershot/Farnborough area, ostensibly to

58

celebrate a reunion of ex-tank crews of the Army of the Rhine, in case there were men of little faith amongst them who would shirk at the prospect of an election.

For a while, Oliver toyed with the idea of asking Rebecca Flemington to make the necessary catering arrangements for the reunion, but in time he realized that this might upset the Army wives who had played such a vital role in the Housing Campaign by petitioning Whitehall on their own. There was another reason for refraining and that was Rebecca's long-standing friendship with Colonel Wallace. In a sense, Rebecca was the Colonel's protégée. In inviting her to take an active part in the organisation of the bogus reunion, Oliver felt that he was inducing her to be disloyal to their mutual friend. If a certain degree of coolness had now crept between the two men, their differences of opinion should in no way interfere with her personal relationship with the Colonel. Oliver felt that she needed the colonel, perhaps even more than she herself suspected, as a father substitute or simply as a link with the past in which her father had figured so prominently.

7

Oliver's heart warmed up at the sight of the men who filled the village hall. As he walked through the entrance, the weight of loneliness lifted from his shoulders; it fell almost instantly, though its burden had bowed his back for days like a mantle of lead, and he marvelled at the power of kinship. Yes, these men were his brothers, regardless of rank, custom, or culture; the ties they had in common were stronger than those of blood relations. He felt moved towards them by an overwhelming desire to vindicate their sincerity which had an Arcadian simplicity which he, the better educated man, found endearing. Amongst the faces he recognized there were some he did not know, but features were not important – these men formed a body; they were the limbs of a body that moved corporately, guided by the same motives, the same impulses. In times of war the dangers they faced collectively bound them together, but this was spasmodic; now, in the no-man's-land in which they found themselves, through no fault of their own, the threats they were exposed to were constant; for that reason comradeship welded them permanently.

As he walked forward through the hall, Oliver shook hands with the men who happened to be closest to him. He had not felt so happy for a long time. The atmosphere was congenial without any trace of awkwardness; it seemed as though the social barriers that normally inhibit exchanges between men of different backgrounds had come down. Without seeming to, Oliver searched the assembly for Sergeant Bates. The attendance was so good that it took him a long time to push his way through to the spot where Sergeant Bates was standing. He could not have missed him, for he was in the company of an even taller man, who wore a faded red beret and carried an accordion. As Oliver approached, intrigued by the para-trooper's appearance, Sergeant Bates motioned the man forward and Oliver was then able to appreciate the full measure of his stature. It was, to say the least, impressive, but the most striking thing about him was the length of his face and the size of his smile – the man was all chin and all smile, and both had an irresistible appeal.

'This is Smiley, Sir,' said Sergeant Bates, 'he's going to play a few tunes for us, if that's all right with you, Sir.'

Smiley beamed. He ran his fingers over the keyboard by way of an introduction and played a few heart-melting chords. His genial manner was so magnetic that it drew attention, by sharp contrast, to the shabbiness of his attire. Oliver wondered why Fortune had not smiled on someone who could smile as kindly as Smiley. Where was the flaw in the man's character, he wondered? To try and find an answer he kept stealing glances at Smiley, search-ing his face.

'Where did you find him?' Oliver asked Sergeant Bates, turning his back on Smiley.

'Outside the Salvation Army, Sir. He had a dog with him. He was playing one old tune after another. You know, "Pack up your Troubles" and "It's a Long Way to Tipperary", all my grandfather's favourites. He seemed to pour his heart out. I asked him if he'd come along to the Reunion and play a few tunes for us and he said "yes". I hope you don't mind, Sir.'

'Of course not, Sergeant. See that he gets this,' Oliver said, pulling a twenty pound note out of his wallet.

'Yes, Sir. Thank you, Sir. He'll appreciate this. He doesn't like the rat race in Civvy Street. He was in the Paras, you see. He tried working as a mercenary for a while, in South America . . . .'

'Well, yes, that'll do, Sergeant.' Oliver would have liked to ask Sergeant Bates to get rid of the charismatic musician right away, but finally compassion prevailed. It was obvious that the man was happy to be in congenial company, amongst his own kind; his being asked to play for comrades had for a few moments interrupted the distasteful course of his life, such as it might be.

The opening bars of an old war lilt suddenly burst out on the assembly. In a trice the chatter that had filled the hall died down and in the hush which ensued, the melody of a popular refrain took possession of every chord in every man's heart, leaving space for nothing but the most uncontrollable emotion. The music made by Smiley's inspired fingers lifted them all into a realm where mundane cares had no place. Oliver was mesmerized. That Smiley's hands had such power, could command such attention, that they could sway the feelings of other men so completely, when perhaps the genial smile that accompanied the music was nothing but an artful gimmick, a natural endowment that Smiley exploited shamelessly for theatrical effects, in a thoroughly reckless way, bewildered him. Whatever the reason, his influence was real, very real, and once seen at work could not easily be forgotten. The whole hall now echoed with the strains of 'If You Were the Only Girl in the World'. There was no stopping the men. All the worries that had depressed them lately, all the fears the future held for them, vanished and they sang, liberating their spirits, putting their hearts and souls into every word of a song their fathers' fathers had sung before them.

Oliver wondered whether or not to give up the idea of addressing the men. The speech he had in mind would come as an anticlimax after Smiley's music-making; it would bring the men down to earth with an awful smack. On the other hand, the reunion had been organized for the sole purpose of the speech, another occasion might not present itself for some time and then it might be too late. Strike the iron . . . Oliver thought. If he could pull it off, if he could manage to take advantage of the men's emotional receptiveness, then the unplanned entertainment would turn to his advantage and, having got through to the men at white heat, there would be no opportunity for recantation when the rapture faded.

A salvo of applause marked the end of Smiley's interlude on the accordion. Triumphantly the men led him to the bar.

'All drinks are on me, Sergeant!' shouted Oliver above the din. Smiley turned round and gave Oliver one of his most bewitching smiles. The man had charisma, there was no denying it, but what lay behind that cordial front? The power to work miracles through music, whence did it come? Oliver did not have time to puzzle long over the enigma of Smiley's persona. He heard a voice behind him.

'Where's the monkey?' It was Rebecca Flemington! She was pointing at Smiley who was being treated at the bar, his accordion still slung over his shoulder.

'HE HATH A DOG,' enunciated Oliver, 'so I am told. That's right, Sergeant, isn't it?'

'Yes, Sir, he has a dog, a little Jack Russell, called Slim,' replied Sergeant Bates who had broken away from the cluster round the bar to await Oliver's orders.

Rebecca burst out laughing.

'Really, you men!'

Much to his displeasure, Oliver noticed that she had

come with a camera and that annoyed him more than her sarcastic remark about Smiley.

Half guessing his thoughts she said, 'In case you wonder why I'm here, I did a little investigating of my own when your friends told me you had gone to an old boys' reunion. I thought you might care to have mementoes of the meeting, photographic ones, I mean, that's why I've come equipped.'

Oliver took Sergeant Bates apart.

'Get rid of him,' he ordered looking towards the bar.

'Who, Sir?'

'HIM!'

'Oh, I see, Sir, yes, Sir, right away, Sir. I've already given him the money. He said to thank you, Sir.'

Oliver then turned towards Rebecca Flemington and said, 'You've got five minutes and never do this again and don't you dare suggest I pose with the men!'

'Oh, dear,' she replied opening her camera, 'it looks as though I have upset the great Caesar!'

Having got rid of Smiley, Sergeant Bates then quickly asked the men who were standing together at the bar to turn round and face Rebecca Flemington's camera; he could sense the urgency of the situation just by looking surreptitiously at Oliver. The men were by then in a jolly mood. After they had had several photographs taken, they insisted that Rebecca joined them and the sergeant used the camera, then they required a snapshot with Sergeant Bates in their midst, but he was so much taller than any of them that Rebecca in the end had him sitting down and the others half bent over him. Oliver could see Rebecca was exhilarated by the whole thing. She was cracking jokes and tittering with the men. Deep down he did not approve of this. He found her behaviour unbecoming and felt sadness rather than amusement at the indecorous way she was disporting herself. It was clear to him that she was used to that kind of fooling and that acting the way she did meant nothing to her: it was part of the professional game she played, a stock-in-trade. All the same, he would have liked her to be a little less flippant, a little bit more self-composed. Coolly he escorted her to the door.

'Are you still cross with me?' she asked, giving him one of her wide thin-lipped smiles.

He shrugged his shoulders. She could think what she liked.

'Goodbye Rebecca.'

Smiling impudently she swung her bag over her shoulder.

'Goodbye Major!'

After he had seen her off, he closed both doors and turned round to go back in. He took a few steps forward; they were hesitant steps as though all the mischief in the world weighed them down to distract him from his purpose. He had not imagined that he would have to exert so much will-power to give them back their spring. From a distance, as he plodded along, he saw Corporal Nash and Sergeant Bates re-establishing order in the hall; it gave him heart. The men watched him get closer. A sheepish look came over their faces. Now the lark was over, they felt embarrassed at having let themselves go in front of someone who had held the rank of an officer. Contrition subdued them. For Oliver it meant that they were just in the right frame of mind to receive his speech. He waited till they were all sitting on the floor round him, then he began.

'I know how disappointed you all were when the housing deal fell through. A lot of you feel unwanted and forgotten. This is why I thought I would ask you to join me here today to try and boost your morale. What you have suffered during your quest for proper homes is only a setback, not a defeat. Your request for decent living standards was a legitimate one and one which no self-respecting nation should ignore when it is made by its soldiers. By rejecting the Council's offer of improper accommodation you expressed your refusal to lay your children open to contamination by drugs, by vandalism, by political bigotry. Through that refusal you claimed the right to obey the dictates of your conscience. You claimed the right to live as free men, unoppressed by the evils of a materialistic society; for you to accept those evils would mean living in a man-made hell. Unfortunately, that right has been ignored; your moral standards have been ignored, because they are not the moral standards accepted by the majority. I put it to you, my friends, which is better: to muddle through in a man-made hell with the majority, or to establish heaven on earth in our own compounds for our children's sake? I know, we all know, that the obstacles which stand between us and that heaven are numerous and dreadful to contemplate; fear strikes in our hearts at the very thought of them. We need courage to face them, but the courage we were asked to call upon as soldiers in the line of duty will not be great enough to enable us to overcome those obstacles. We must develop another kind of courage for which there is no model. It is not always easy to exercise courage along the lines decreed by conventional warfare, but to exercise it in a conflict where one constantly faces the unknown is a hundred times more difficult. It takes exceptional courage to call one's countrymen one's enemies. It takes exceptional courage not to flinch in the face of an adversary who yesterday was our equal in the eyes of the law. The question you must ask yourselves is which will be easier, to muster that kind of exceptional courage as individuals waging isolated actions or united under one leadership, bearing in mind that you will be fighting to safeguard the safety of the innocent? Now I will leave you to decide for yourselves which it'll be.'

Visibly moved, Sergeant Bates broke away from the men.

'Wait, Sir,' he said.

'I'll wait outside,' came Oliver's firm reply. 'Let them cast votes.'

Within a very short space of time Sergeant Bates was back.

'Well, Sergeant, what's the verdict?'

'United under one leadership, Sir.'

'Was the verdict unanimous?'

'Unanimous, Sir,' replied Sergeant Bates, nodding his head to confirm his reply.

Then Oliver asked 'Whose leadership?'

'Yours, Sir.'

'Very well, Sergeant, but I want the men to pledge solidarity.'

Oliver walked back into the hall followed by Sergeant Bates. When the men saw him coming, they stood to attention.

'Stand at ease,' Oliver commanded them. 'I have come to accept your leadership in the spirit of a new brotherhood, not in the formal capacity of a Major. I thank you all for your trust. To fulfil the task you have entrusted me with, I need each one of you to pledge solidarity. Will you do it?'

Corporal Nash instantly joined Sergeant Bates. Both soldiers looked at each other, and then at the men; lifted their right arm and said, 'Solidarity!' and the men shouted, 'Solidarity!' after them.

'Till death?' asked Oliver.

'Till death!' replied the men.

8

Mrs Cunningham put down her handbag on the glove drawer, adjusted her pearl choker and tidied up her auburn hair. She was waiting for Miss Beaumont who had gone to the garage to collect the car. Miss Beaumont had been gone a long time, longer than usual, and Mrs Cunningham wondered after a while what was keeping her in the garage. She opened the front door and listened for the sound of the engine being revved up but could not hear anything, not even the slamming of a door. Thinking it was odd, she decided to walk over to the garage to have a look. Maybe Madge had slipped out to give instructions to one of the cleaners at the house before starting the car; she was getting forgetful.

The car was still in the garage. Mrs Cunningham walked round to the front.

'Ah! there you are! I was getting worried,' she said to Miss Beaumont who was sitting at the wheel. 'Have you lost the keys?'

It looked as though Miss Beaumont was reaching for something on the floor; she was slumped across the wheel with her left arm hanging down and her head resting sideways on the wheel; her eyes stared straight ahead of her.

'My God, Madge! What has happened?' Getting no reply, Mrs Cunningham stood still in the garage. Miss

68

Beaumont had of late put on a lot of weight. None of the women who worked at the house, certainly not that wisp in the library, could lift her out of the car; it needed a strong man . . . . Mrs Cunningham started giggling. She gave herself a quick look in the wing mirror, tidied up her hair again and, trying to stifle her giggles in a handker-chief, sauntered out of the garage. As she emerged between the stone pillars that marked the entrance of the property, she saw Oldfield the gardener driving down the road in his mini-tractor. Finding him so quickly was really an incredible piece of luck; she just could not believe her good fortune.

He stopped the tractor when he saw her and stared at her blankly. Tears were running down her face she was giggling so much. She clambered up onto the running board as best she could in her tight tweed skirt.

'What's up?' he asked gruffly.

'She's gone, she's dead.'

'Who's gone?'

'Madge. You've got to help me carry the body into the house.'

'Why? Where is she?'

'In the garage, inside the car.'

Oldfield said nothing for a while, then he lumbered out of the tractor.

'Not till I've had my treat.'

'Don't be silly,' Mrs Cunningham said between giggles. 'Come on, let's not waste any time talking now she's gone . . ..'

'Shouldn't we . . . ?'

'No, later. The old bag can wait, she's had her fling. Now it's my turn. When I think of all the weeks, months, years I've waited.'

'Don't be ungrateful!'

'Oh, I know. In the woodshed on top of log piles, in the

barn on top of greens, with the basket-ball team flashing their beefy thighs on the playing-field outside and the gym mistress's whistle going every two minutes. It's time things changed around here.'

Oldfield pushed Mrs Cunningham into the bungalow.

'Where's the bedroom? Come on! Where is it?'

Mrs Cunningham opened up her largest most bewitching smile.

'Shan't tell you,' she hummed, running round the hall.

'You bloody bitch!' Oldfield flung open all the doors of the bungalow. He was still wearing his gum boots, his grubby wax jacket and his faded tweed cap. 'This is it, then, isn't it?' he asked as he espied a large double bed in one of the rooms. 'It's got to be, the size you are and the size she was.'

Next to the bed there stood a bedside table with a photograph on it of Miss Beaumont wearing a Panama hat and Mrs Cunningham in a sundress. An inscription across it read 'Capri Forever'.

'I'll give you "Capri Forever"!' shouted Oldfield as he swept the photograph off the bedside table with one flick of the hand and sent it flying through the air. Then he bent down and picked up the two pairs of bedroom slippers that were lying side by side in front of the bed and threw them across the room.

'Bull in a china shop . . . ,' tittered Mrs Cunningham. She did not have time to remove her choker. Oldfield grabbed her by the arm and flung her on the bed.

9

Stella had just posted a letter addressed to her mother in Guernsey. She was slowly making her way back to Darley Hall when she saw a shocking sight. Her immediate reaction was to turn round and hurry away from it. Following tracks made by deer, she cut across some woods and soon found her way to the edge of the main drive that led to Darley Hall. Once on the drive, she noticed one of the cleaners who worked at the school pedalling towards the house ahead of her and she hung back. It was not that she disliked the cleaner; she was in fact a superior woman and one of the few people Stella enjoyed chatting to at the school, but today she did not feel like talking to anyone. Not only had she been shocked by what she had just seen on the corner of the main road, but also she was still smarting from her interview with Mrs Cunningham that very morning. The cleaning woman got off her bicycle to take off her crash helmet and, noticing Stella, waited for her to catch up. Stella cursed; she was definitely not in a loquacious mood. Almost against her will she looked down at the ground.

'What's the matter?' asked the cleaner, 'you look upset.'

Stella looked up and kept walking on as she spoke.

'I've just seen . . . I don't know that I ought to tell you . . . Mrs Cunningham at the corner of the main road. She was sitting on a trailer, with her skirt hitched up high above her knees and her legs dangling off the ground. The trailer was full of vegetables. The gardener was leaning against the side of the trailer right up close to her. They were laughing together. It seemed so immodest on her part to expose her knees and thighs on a public highway, especially with him there.'

'Didn't you know? Oh, it's been going on for years though not many people knew about it and now, of course, with Miss Beaumont dead, there is no need to hide.'

'But I thought,' Stella stammered, 'I mean I saw them one day, Miss Beaumont and Mrs Cunningham, quite by chance, as I was passing by . . . Miss Beaumont's study door was ajar. They were kissing.'

'Well, yes, but I think she did it for the money. Miss Beaumont was a very wealthy woman. The gardener is not well off, his crops are too few. He doesn't own any land.'

'But how can she? The man's a boor!'

'You know what it is like nowadays, anything goes. They were all adults, consenting adults. Their private lives were their own affairs. Still it's a wonder that none of the parents who visited the school ever suspected anything . . . . There is such a thing as libel and slander, I suppose. Would you have told your mother if you had found out sooner?'

'Good Lord, no!' exclaimed Stella, 'I could never have brought myself to mention anything like that. My mother would not have believed me anyway. She thought very highly of Mrs Cunningham.'

'You know how it is with parents; they come and go; they have their own problems. Besides, not everybody has a nose for that sort of thing.'

Stella stopped dead in the drive. A name flashed across her memory. Major Carrington! He had a 'nose' for that sort of thing; he had suspected something, he had spoken out. She had been unfair to him!

'Oh, how could I?' Stella moaned aloud.

'What's that, dear?'

'Oh, nothing, I mean, it's terrible to be young, to be unwary. I have been incredibly stupid.'

'Don't be too hard on yourself,' said the cleaner. 'You had your job, your books. We all knew how much the books meant to you.'

'Yes,' Stella assented sadly, 'they were my life, that is probably why I understood so little about what went on around me.'

'Well, the good thing about finding oneself wanting is that one can always make amends. It is not the end of the world,' the cleaner said, winking an eye.

Stella jumped at the idea. Yes, she could make amends, she could write to Major Carrington, she could apologize. The thought gave her wings. For a moment she had a sensation of joy; she felt liberated.

They had almost reached the end of the drive.

'I have something else to tell you,' Stella said to the cleaner, 'I shall be leaving shortly. Mrs Cunningham gave me notice first thing this morning.'

'Good heavens, child! What will you do?'

'I don't know . . . go home for a while, I suppose. Then look for another training post.'

'I'm ever so sorry. What on earth made her do a thing like that?'

'I don't think she liked me very much.'

'Perhaps she thought you got on too well with Miss Beaumont.'

'Perhaps, but I think it's something else. I think she knew I saw them that day in the study; it was too close to home for comfort.'

'It's just as well, then, I'm a great believer in divine

providence. I always think those things happen for the best, don't you?'

Stella wished she could have inclined to the same rose-coloured view, but at that precise moment she could only deplore the inconvenience of this turn of events. She sighed.

'All the same, it's a damned nuisance. I'll come and say goodbye before I leave.'

'Yes, do. You know where I live, the little cottage next door to the village store. I expect I'll see you up at the school. There's still a lot of tidying up to do in there. Take care!'

Stella shook her head and smiled. That she would!

*　　*　　*

Stella took a sheet of paper and sat down. What had seemed an idea fraught with therapeutic virtues, now that she had to put pen to paper, turned out to be a punishing task. She felt both numb and wayward. As she sat staring at the blank page in front of her, she realized she had been carried away by the cleaning woman's simple-minded optimism. Enthusiastically, on the spur of the moment, she had imagined it would be easy to write to Major Carrington, making a clean breast of it. Now faced with the execution she felt inhibited. The idea of offering an apology to Major Carrington in 'cold blood' in a letter which he would receive 'out of the blue' proved more and more distasteful; what made her finally reject it was the knowledge that by confessing she would be laying her soul bare to him and that she could not bring herself to do. All she was prepared to say was that she had been dismissed from her post. By way of an introduction, she would remind him that he had offered his help if ever she needed it. To this solution she assented fully and with a sense of relief. Once or twice, though, the awkwardness she would

74

create if eventually she did meet him again face to face, by hiding from him the initial motive behind the letter, presented itself to her in the form of a flash of intuition, but it was too short-lived for her to be deeply bothered by it; she was able to dismiss it from her mind and posted the letter in its spurious form.

*   *   *

That Oliver could be deceived by the feint of Stella's letter was just another proof of her ingenuousness. He had been right about her – she was vulnerable – to him her letter was transparent: she had found out about Darley Hall and she wanted him to know. In the few very short moments Oliver had spent in Stella's company, he had understood that the key to her character was its secretiveness, born of pride; even when faced with his 'snake pit' tactics, as he called them, she had remained immured in proud reserve. Maybe she had been shocked into silence and that had made her more reticent, more determined not to mention the scandalous trauma, the depth of which could only be measured in relation to the high ideals he suspected she held. For her to come out of her silence must have been hard enough; to expect that simultaneously she would reveal what had moved her to write was fanciful. All the same, she had written, and that represented a first attempt to knock on the wall she had built round herself; like a prisoner whose tap-tapping echoes faintly through the thickness of stone, she had signalled. He was rather pleased about that. After all, as she had rightly pointed out, they were perfect strangers. It could also mean she had no-one else to turn to. His heart felt compassion at the thought of her isolation, but this grievous mood did not last long. There were practical arrangements to be made before he could answer her letter. Her horse would have to be moved; it was unlikely that she would want him to stay in the area and she herself would have to be put up not too far away from the horse. The friends he was staying with in Aldershot had given him the only spare room in the house; besides he did not know of any livery stables nearby. Much as he disliked the idea, he might have to mention the problem to Rebecca Flemington to see if she could help to find temporary accommodation for Stella.

He was undecided about this for some time. The two women had never met. He doubted whether they even knew about each other's existence. He could not remember having mentioned Stella's name to Rebecca. Above all, he feared Rebecca's sarcastic remarks which he felt sure she would let fly. He could never picture her in his mind without the camera she carried over her shoulder transforming itself into a quiver.

*   *   *

'I must say, Major, that you are full of surprises. I am sure the tank is to blame, as a place of concealment, I mean. Who's to know what goes on behind that armour-plated hood? And when is this blue-stocking arriving in our midst, or is that another one of your well-guarded secrets?'

Oliver looked at Rebecca dispassionately.

'Nothing has been arranged as yet.'

'But no doubt it will be as soon as it can be manoeuvred and engineered. What about Colonel Wallace, has he come up with any suggestions? Couldn't he put her up for a while?'

'Rebecca, I don't think you understand the problem. I am asking you as a female.'

'Aren't you being a little old-fashioned? I mean things have changed since you joined the Army.'

'Why upset the sensitivities of a young girl who is not particularly with it?'

'Well, perhaps she needs toughening up.'

'No, she doesn't, quite the opposite,' Oliver replied firmly. 'What she needs is gentling.'

Rebecca looked at him, smiling.

'One of those, is she? It's amazing how some women get away with it, I mean appealing to the male's protective instinct; my mother did . . . she found a man who fell for that sort of stuff. It's not given to everyone . . . ,' her voice trailed off with contained emotion, 'I'm sorry, I didn't mean to . . . .'

'To what?'

'To criticize you . . . Who am I to criticize you?'

Oliver thought he would gain nothing by carrying on the conversation. It had been a mistake to turn to Rebecca for help in such a delicate matter. He apologized for having disturbed her. An area of his life had to remain closed to her; perhaps it was just as well.

10

The horse walked straight up the ramp of the horsebox and started pulling at the hay-net Stella had hung for him inside.

'Well, that's that,' said Oliver who was anxious to expedite the business of Stella's departure from Darley Hall. He had found her tense when he arrived. She had smiled nervously, avoiding his eyes and said very little. Her luggage stood in a pile outside the porch ready to be picked up. As they walked round to the house, Stella looked up one last time at her bedroom window under the roof. Sweeping the facade her eye caught sight of Mrs Cunningham standing behind the curtains of Miss Beaumont's study on the first floor.

'She's watching us,' she told Oliver.

'Who is?'

'Mrs Cunningham; it gives me the creeps.'

'You have said goodbye?' enquired Oliver.

'Oh, yes. She was in Miss Beaumont's study, sitting in Miss Beaumont's chair . . . . She told me Miss Beaumont had left her everything, including Darley Hall. It was horrible. She was gloating over her riches.' Stella paused and then went on. 'She asked me who you were.'

'What did you say?'

'I said you had been in the Army . . . . She then asked me if you were the same person who had called round at

78

the bungalow a few weeks ago and I said yes, you were
. . . .'

'She didn't like that,' Oliver put in, hazarding a guess.

'She said I was taking a chance going with you. You
were weird. Miss Beaumont, who had a sixth sense, had
told her you were weird.'

'Really? And what do you think?'

'I don't know . . . . Maybe you are weird.'

Oliver laughed and, still laughing, looked up at the
study window. Stella, who followed his gaze, saw Mrs
Cunningham withdrawing sharply behind the curtains.
Well, that was it! Quickly, she climbed into the horsebox
while Oliver picked up the bags she had left in front of the
porch. Through the window she watched him storing
them carefully in the cab with the horse's paraphernalia.
She noted that he had a quiet and efficient way of
handling stuff which she found confidence-giving. It
showed that he was in control, not only of material
objects, which he manipulated with precision, but also of
the situation as a whole; though to her that situation was
precarious, his behaviour gave it positiveness and made it
less uncertain for her to accept. He had vaguely told her
where she was going . . . . The arrangements made for her
horse she found satisfactory . . . . As the box started
pulling out of the drive, she reflected not without anguish
that she had learnt to cope with her personal situation at
Darley Hall through constant practice. The effort had
engaged her wits so thoroughly that she wondered if she
could turn to the management of an entirely different set
of circumstances with the same desperate application.
The movement of the horsebox on the road soon lulled her
doubt away and she fell asleep, exhausted.

*   *   *

Oliver had just got back to his friends' in Aldershot

after dropping off Stella and her horse at their destinations when the telephone rang. It was Sergeant Bates requesting a word with the Major.

'You sound worried, Sergeant. Is there a problem?'

'Yes, Sir, there is. It's the wives, mine and a lot of others . . . .'

'Don't you think you'd better come round to the house and explain?'

'Oh, yes, Sir.'

Face to face with Oliver, Sergeant Bates disclosed what the matter was. After the reunion at the Village Hall, the men had gone home and told their wives everything. Alarmed by the implications of Oliver's speech to their husbands, the women thought they would set about obtaining their just desires by sensible means. They drafted another petition, intended for the King's Consort this time, because they thought that as a wife, a mother and a home-maker, the Queen was far more likely to lend a sympathetic ear to their plea for good homes than a government department. Remembering the failure of their wives' first petition, the men had tried to discourage them, but to no avail: they were dead set on it.

'Pity,' Oliver said, 'they'll be disappointed. The other thing is, it's doubtful a gang of women turning up at the Palace to present a petition to the King's Consort will attract media attention. What is needed now is a protest march, a rally on a bigger scale, including women and children, well-organized and well-publicised to attract the attention of all the media. Then one might reasonably expect results.'

'There's no stopping them, Sir,' insisted Sergeant Bates, 'they're sold on the idea. You know women . . . .'

'Do I? I wonder . . . .' Oliver asked himself privately. Rebecca Flemington's character still presented posers. Stella's he found less cryptic.

'Well, if it makes them happy.'

'Oh, it'll do that all right, Sir.'

'You must let them go ahead, Sergeant, you have no alternative.'

After he had led Sergeant Bates to the door, Oliver stayed on the doorstep a while, staring at the tall gaunt figure whose gait he noticed was less elastic than it had been. Thoughts raced through his mind. At the reunion in the Village Hall he had got the men to pledge solidarity; what he should have done was to swear them to secrecy as well . . . The wives would have to be admonished, the sooner the better. Wise after the event, he went indoors and started right away to gather the threads of the Remonstrance he would draft and eventually issue to the women to make them see sense.

Mrs Bates took delivery of the Remonstrance late in the evening of the following day and, having gone through the text several times to assure herself she was not dreaming, she called her neighbours in and read them the amazing document.

The Remonstrance

'We are often told by well-meaning people wishing to enlighten us that "Religion is the opium of the people". This may well be the case abroad but in this country, I say to you, in this country, Royalty is the opium of the people. As a nation we are addicted to Royalty; we are intoxicated by Royalty. The habit makes us incapable of rational thought; it deprives us of volition and, what is worse, renders us oblivious of the situation in which we have fallen through the loss both of judgement and free will. Now, while we perpetuate that senseless condition down the generations, there reigns over us a monarch with manifold attributes. We have above us a "fountain of justice", a "fountain of honour", a "defender of the Faith", a "commander-in-chief of all the armed forces", a patron of the arts, a leader of society, in other words an incomparable being. Not unnaturally, we wish to continue in the practice of an addiction which keeps us in a state of somnolent subservience to this glorious embodiment.

'Who will deliver us from addictiveness? Who will give us back our critical faculties? Be prepared for a shock! The Sovereign Himself will do that for us! For no narcotic will now sublimate the vision of a royal image tarnished by public scandal, elevate moral standards that have been debased by an autocratic code of conduct. How often in the past have we heard the slogan, "In this country we need Royalty to look up to!" To look up to, not to look down on! Never, at any time during our history has kingship guaranteed the honorability of the monarch as a figurehead, but even less so now when Pressmen can with impunity let loose the Hounds of Heaven just anywhere. What did the King hope for? That he could expose himself to the media for his own ends and not be judged? That the bark of the Hounds of Heaven would not echo through the royal chamber and percolate down to the dens of the opium-eaters? "Privilege" we cry, as in olden time, if that is the case.

"It is time to speak plain English." Your husbands as soldiers were asked to swear allegiance to the Crown, thus forfeiting their lives for king and country. What have they been given in exchange? Not Charity (they are still homeless) yet the King is "defender of the Faith" and Charity, we know, is the essential virtue of our Faith; not Justice (they are still jobless) yet the King is the "Fountain of Justice", and least of all Honour from the "Fountain of Honour". There is no honour attached to being thrown out in a heap on Civvy Street after years of service; there is no honour in being unwanted in one's own country; there is no honour in being forgotten in one's own country, as though one had never been bound to it by oath and never been prepared to suffer the fatal consequence of the oath, shedding one's blood.

'If the oath of allegiance meant that by taking it your husbands entered into a contract with the Crown, then I say to you that contract is null and void – the King, not them, has broken it. The trust they placed in Him as a most excellent figurehead, trusting Him to act morally and ethically at all times, that trust has been breached and they are no longer morally contracted. It is with the people of England that your husbands must enter into a new type of contract, a social contract, and it is to the people of England that YOU must turn, to its perennial goodwill and good humour, to claim your right.

'Now you can see your course with clarity.'

Oliver Carrington

Few were the Army wives who were not demoralized by the Remonstrance after they had digested its contents. To the excitement that surrounded the drafting of their petition to the Queen, and the bustle that attended the collection of signatures for it, succeeded apathy. The fact that the petition turned out to be a complete waste of time seemed to count for nothing compared with the thrill of having stood at the Palace gate. The Remonstrance ushered in an anticlimax, to which the wives reacted in different ways. Some withdrew within themselves to brood over a feeling of futility; they went about their daily chores like automata; others 'carried on' about the harm the Remonstrance had done to their dignity, blaming their husbands for letting Major Carrington give them 'a rap on the knuckles, like kids at school'. The men pleaded ignorance. They asked if they might be allowed to take a look at the Remonstrance. Tactlessly, many of them approved of it and told their wives so, thereby pouring fuel over the fire. Not knowing how to restore peace in their homes, a few of them suggested consulting the Major for advice; the idea was immediately rejected by a majority.

'What do you want to do, then?' asked Sergeant Bates, peeved by the men's attitude. 'You know nobody gives a sh . . . about our affairs. The Major is the only person who's ever shown an interest.'

Many evenings were spent in heated arguments. Eventually, under sufferance, a group of men followed Sergeant Bates to Oliver's friends' house. Oliver was very pleased to hear that the Remonstrance had had the desired effect on the women – it had sobered them up. Now that they had their feet on the ground, the wives could be steered in the right direction and the greatest hopes of success entertained. The men shook their heads. It was all very well, but their home life was not very happy and their wives' moods were having an adverse effect on the children. Oliver thought that he had better

84

come up with an idea. The answer to their problem, he told them, was a woman: not an Army wife, another woman, an outsider. Only another woman would know how to nurse their wives' wounded vanity and he knew the right person for the job. He would send Rebecca Flemington to them. She would give their wives something new to think about; she would harness their energies into a constructive channel this time.

'You all know General Flemington's daughter. She'll deal with your matrimonial problems very ably, I think. Your wives will be true helpmates again, I promise you.'

*　　*　　*

Rebecca took a quick look round the room where the Army wives were gathered and immediately realized that she was not welcome; they were all sulking. Not being the sort of person to be put off by disgruntled faces (in her profession she often had to humour difficult clients), she started pulling out of two large portfolios some black and white prints.

'These are the photographs I took at Major Carrington's request on the night that he and some of your husbands carried out a reconnaissance tour of the highrise flats on the Copeland Estate. As you will see in a minute, these photographs are the tangible results of an investigation with special aims. This print, for instance, deals with a sanitation problem which is unusual in blocks of flats with modern conveniences.'

A few giggles met Rebecca's words as she held up high in front of her a shot of a urine-stained angle between two walls.

'This one deals with the problem of drug-peddling which is rife on the estate.'

Exclamations went up as Rebecca lifted in the air the

85

print with cast-off syringes, the one Oliver admired amongst all others.

'Look at that!' 'Smashing!' 'No other word for it' 'Have you any more like it, Miss?'

'Oh, yes,' replied Rebecca, 'lots more. Would you like to see them? But I must warn you, some of them require a strong stomach, and please call me Rebecca.'

'We ought to see them all, don't you think?' asked Mrs Bates, turning to the other women.

'Yes, definitely,' replied Corporal Nash's wife. 'We've all heard dreadful tales about the flats, but seeing is believing. We might as well know the worst.'

Rebecca smiled. It had not taken long to bring the women round. She had not been too happy in the first place about taking on this conciliatory task; it was reassuring to see the women responding so quickly. As she pulled print after print out of the portfolios and laid them on the floor for the women to look at, she let the personal thoughts that pre-occupied her drift through her mind, dropping an absent-minded 'yes' or 'really' as the women commented on the photographic evidence of the more sordid aspects of life on the Copeland Estate. She had never before been in such an unstable emotional state. Her work suffered from it. Every day as she opened her studio door, she was greeted by a backlog of work which she could expedite, if she set her mind to it. A lack of confidence seemed to be at the root of the problem. Why, mystified her. The only thing that she had felt confident about lately was her snap decision to refuse to find accommodation for Oliver's 'waif' – that area of his life had to remain his and his alone. She had all the more reason for congratulating herself on having reacted quickly since his request had instilled blind panic in her, and still did at times, when she remembered it. To allay this panic, she liked to think the great God Pan had had one of his pranks at her expense in one of his lighter moments.

From the very beginning. she had decided to keep her relationship with Carrington on a semi-professional basis. That stance enabled her to run the gamut between sarcasm and mockery, modulating as she went along; the safe keeping of her freedom depended on it; and it was fun. Oddly, lately the fun had turned sour. She was not so sure any more about the soundness of her attitude. Questioning the initial motive which fashioned the attitude did not worry her; everybody made mistakes, starting from the wrong premise. What bothered her was the growing suspicion that the query had something to do with Stella. Had Stella not appeared on the scene, would she have carried on blithely as before, or would the independence game have proved hollow by now just the same? Why Stella? Stella was a bookworm; she was dull, at least that was the impression she gave. She had only met Stella once. When Carrington asked her to come round to the house in Aldershot to find out if she would try and humour his henchmen's wives and prepare them for the protest march, Stella was there. Apart from a brief 'hello', Stella never said a word. She just stood there in her drab clothes looking lost. There did not appear to be a spark of life in her. Oliver behaved as though she were part of the furniture, talking openly in front of her. Rebecca coughed once or twice, casting quizzical looks in Stella's direction, but Oliver ignored her silent queries and carried on talking. Was it a coincidence? Was Stella dumb anyway, or had she been ordered to keep quiet by Oliver? Now she herself was actually engaged in doing what Oliver asked for – bringing the women round – she wondered if she had accepted to do Oliver's bidding simply because Stella was in the room. If that were the case, if her decision had been influenced by Stella's presence, then she had been taken advantage of by a trick of Machiavellian cunning, and that hurt.

She looked anxiously at the women around her, hoping nothing in her exterior had given away her perplexed state of mind. The women had finished looking at the prints; they were lifting them off the floor. With a sigh of relief Rebecca opened the portfolios and showed the women how to drop the prints carefully inside between sheets of protective film. Cups of tea were being handed round; it was time to finish the business.

'I expect you all know the plans for the protest march are going ahead. The prints you have just looked at will be enlarged poster-size and mounted on shanks, to be carried high above the procession. What Major Carrington wants you to do is to write a placard for each picture. Only you can do that in the full knowledge of your personal situation as wives and mothers. Are any of you good at writing?'

'Vera is,' said one of the women, turning round to the rear of the group. You keep a day-to-day diary, don't you, Vera?'

'Have done so for the past twelve years, every single night, me dear.'

'Right, Vera,' said Rebecca. 'See what you can come up with – keep the captions short, short and pungent, real punch lines. Don't forget that you'll be moving forward all the time and the slogans must stick in people?s minds long after the procession's gone. If any of you have ideas, pass them on to Vera and discuss them with her. Well, goodbye and good luck!'

Rebecca put down her cup of tea and picked up her two portfolios. She thought they felt heavier than when she first arrived.

'God, I'm tired, tired and depressed.' She got into her

car but, driving with no-one in the passenger seat, there was nothing to distract her from the thoughts that tumbled relentlessly through her mind in a downward spiral. What on earth did Oliver see in Stella? was one of the questions that plagued her. Apart from having a nice figure, she was colourless and lifeless. Maybe that was the chink in Oliver's armour: he had a taste for dummies! (Come to think of it, she had often wondered where the loophole was.) The surmise was not very flattering. She would have preferred him with a foible for glamour, a leaning towards wit and beauty. Instead of being demeaned by his dubious inclination towards the nondescript, she could have basked in the reflection of his commendable taste and not felt disappointed in him. With the protest march in the offing and all the preparations that went with it, plus the prospect of its consequence, which might be far-reaching, someone like Stella could prove a dead weight, an encumbrance; she looked so helpless. What would Oliver do with her in tow if his attempt to foment public opinion succeeded and trouble broke out? Stella was unsuitable. What Oliver needed . . . .

Rebecca saw the traffic lights changing and applied the brakes just in time; it had been a close thing! She didn't think that she had been carried away by her imagination into thinking . . . . There were certain signs . . . . For one thing, her photographs of the Copeland Estate were an integral part of the protest march; most probably the impact of the march would come from them, provided the Army wives did their homework well. She could make herself indispensable to the movement in many different ways, not simply as a photographer . . . . She did have nearly all the requisites for an appointment . . . . Supposing she did throw her lot in with Oliver, what had she got to lose? She had reached the pinnacle of her profession; her parents were dead; she had no family ties . . . . As for Wallace, what had he ever done for her? He was just an old fool, a windbag. She could not understand why she had bothered to keep in touch with him all those years.

11

Stella was on her way to bed for an early night when she heard Pandora calling from the hall. Rather than be impolite to her hostess, she turned back and reached the hall in time to see Pandora kicking off her fashion boots as she was wont to do after a long day spent modelling in London.

'Oh, hello, Stella! Sorry I couldn't let you know when I'd be back. I've had the hell of a day. I'm parched. Is there any milk in the fridge?'

'I'm not sure. I've been out all I day myself.'

'Oh. I thought it was your turn this week to keep an eye on supplies. Not to worry. How did it go, your day out?'

'I had a couple of interviews. One of them was in London.'

'Any good?'

'I don't know. I can't make up my mind about either of them . . . .'

'Maybe you're being too choosy . . . .'

'Well, if you'd rather I went . . . .'

'I didn't mean it that way! of course, you can stay here as long as you like. It's just that I'm out all day and so is the other girl. You're going to get bored if you don't take a job soon. I know I would, I like being busy.'

'Yes, you do, don't you?' whispered Stella who felt exhausted just thinking about Pandora's hectic schedule.

'What about bananas? Have we got any? I'm starving.'

'Yes, one.'

'Right! A banana, preferably with a glass of milk.'

'Aren't you afraid of getting fat . . . I mean for your job?' asked Stella.

'Have you ever modelled ski clothes under artificial sunlight?' asked Pandora. 'I must have lost pounds today, perspiring under fake fur. I'm not complaining; I love it! One day it's swimsuits in Hyde Park by the Serpentine with ducks skidding off the ice in arctic temperatures; another day it's mountaineering gear in Spain in the blistering heat.'

As she spoke, Pandora finished taking off her leather clothes. 'But I wouldn't want to do anything else. I like the work, I like the people I meet, I have a lot of fun . . .'

When Stella came back from the kitchen carrying a tray with a banana and a glass of milk, Pandora was in the middle of the sitting-room floor in her black body suit ready to do her work-out to music. She looked rather splendid in a body suit; it showed off her figure and her blonde curly hair, which she wore very long in a natural style.

'Do you ever relax?' Stella asked, amazed anybody should have so much energy.

'This is my way of relaxing. You ought to try it some time.'

'I mean, do you ever relax with a book, quietly?'

'Only when I'm at sea. I love reading at sea. Don't you?'

'I don't know. I've only ever been on a Channel Island ferry and usually I'm too sick to do anything, let alone read a book.'

'Oh, you won't be sick on the *Amaryllis*! Dr Fanshawe will see to that. He'll give you something.'

The news floored Stella. 'The *Amaryllis*! but that's a

flower.'

'No, it's a yacht! You'll love her! She's sailed round the world, you know. A book has been written about her. There is a copy of it on a shelf in Dr Fanshawe's cabin.'

'What is it called?' asked Stella faintly.

'*The Cruise of the Amaryllis.* It makes fascinating reading.'

'I wish you would explain, Pandora. I've had two interviews; it's enough for one day.'

'It was meant to be a surprise. It's Camilla's long weekend off, she flies back from Bali tomorrow, and Oliver Carrington told my aunt that you needed cheering up, so I thought, as Dr Fanshawe invited us for the weekend, I mean, Camilla and I, I thought you could come as well, rather than stay in the flat by yourself. He owns the *Amaryllis.*'

'I can't! Thank you very much for having thought of me, but I can't. I've got to look after my horse.'

'Don't be such a stick-in-the-mud! Somebody else can do the horse. I'm sure Oliver could arrange it, if you asked him. He could send one of his men; they'd welcome the chance.'

'I don't know. Maybe. I'll have to think about it; I'll let you know later.'

'You don't have to decide now, this minute. Dr Fanshawe always has crowds of people staying anyway. It just seems a pity to miss such a fabulous opportunity.'

'I really must go to bed, it's been a long day.'

The strains of syncopated music soon thrummed through Stella's melancholy reflections. Her well-ordered life at Darley Hall, the hours she spent quietly reading, the meals at regular times, all that appeared to belong to some mythological past from which she had been separated by aeons. Pandora's modelling jobs made any kind of routine impossible.

Stella began to regret not having gone to Guernsey to stay with her mother, not just because Pandora was a niece of Major Carrington's friends, an inconvenience if ever there was one – it meant he could indirectly keep an eye on her – but mostly because Pandora's life-style made her feel uncomfortable. At this point, Stella remarked, not without self-mockery, that her decision not to go to her mother's in Guernsey had been made to avoid discomfort! She knew, she could never bring herself to disclose to her mother in detail the events which had led to her dismissal from Darley Hall. She felt that the disclosure of those unsavoury facts would desecrate their relationship. On the other hand, keeping all those secrets from her mother, as she firmly intended to do, was bound to create an awkwardness between them. Her mother was a sensitive person; she would sense the lack of ease and wonder what made Stella diffident. But Stella was adamant; she could not give verbal expression to anything that offended her modesty. She believed that, given utterance, the offensive matter would proliferate, whereas kept in the dark fastness of conscience, not brought into the sweet light of daily living on the all-powerful wings of speech, it would languish for a while and eventually die . . . . She had sent her mother the briefest of notes, just telling her Miss Beaumont had died suddenly and as a result she had lost her job, adding that she was too busy looking for another post to come home just yet.

Though her feeling ill-at-ease with Pandora had nothing to do with the strain of secrecy – Stella had no reason to be open with Pandora – nevertheless tension hovered between them, and the sensation was not particularly pleasant. Now to complicate matters, there was this nautical weekend looming . . . . How like Pandora to spring a surprise of that magnitude on one! Pandora thought nothing of sauntering off, not attaching very

94

much importance to why or with whom or where, so long as she was decked in fashion clothes and fun was allied to glamour. It seemed unlikely it ever dawned on her that other people had different values and would not necessarily be gratified by what she enjoyed. But, of course, Pandora had meant to be kind to her by asking her to join the party aboard the *Amaryllis* . . . .

If word came and she was offered one of the posts she had applied for, Stella thought she would accept the position, especially if it meant going to London.

12

The *Amaryllis* was the most signal example of maritime beauty Stella had ever set eyes on. She lay at anchor on the furthermost stretch of water beyond the marina. Other crafts were anchored offshore forward of her anchorage and a very pleasant sight they were, bobbing up and down with the lapping of the water, but of all the vessels that enlivened the scene, the *Amaryllis* was, to Stella's eyes, the most impressive. She was well-proportioned; this harmony gave her elegant lines, shown off to advantage by the distance which separated her from the other yachts. Whereas the boats that rode at anchor nearby were black or brown, she was white. In the failing light her whiteness took on deepening shades of blues and greys; these brought her outline into hard focus and conferred on her a bulk with majestic presence.

The sound of the oars on the water accompanied Stella's contemplation of the *Amaryllis*, coaxing it, rocking it so that both the gentle swaying of the yacht tugging at anchor and the striking of the oars at lazy intervals merged into one musical spell. As the rowing boat made the final lap to the anchorage and the *Amaryllis* came into full view, Stella had no difficulty in believing the yacht had circumnavigated the globe; she had that capable air about her. Just to look at the *Amaryllis* one knew she could tackle anything. Stella turned towards Pandora, who was busy waving her scarf at someone on board.

'Did Dr Fanshawe sail the *Amaryllis* round the world?'

'No, he bought her after she had completed her trip. He became besotted with her when she came home. He said she was like a beautiful woman who has had many lovers. She had left her maiden voyage far behind her and that made her more interesting. So he bought her!'

Stella noticed that there were a lot of people already on board; they were calling the girls and telling them to hurry up.

'How did you meet him?' asked Stella.

'Who? Dr Fanshawe?'

'Yes . . . .'

'Oh, it was fate, really,' Pandora replied, picking up her overnight case. 'The Agency I work for asked me to model some cruise wear; they said they had hired a yacht in Cowes for the occasion from a doctor . . . .'

'The *Amaryllis*?'

'Yes, how did you guess?!'

While Dr Fanshawe's young man steered the rowing boat to the bottom of the gangway, Stella stole a look at the harbour. All the lights round it had been turned on and to the rear of it windows were beginning to light up. It was a wonderful sight.

'Come on, Stella!' shouted Pandora, who had already alighted on the bottom tread of the gangway.

Stella followed her unsteadily. As she climbed, she noticed a middle-aged man in shorts standing at the top of the gangway. By the time she reached the deck, the man was putting his arms round Pandora's and Camilla's waists and was hugging them both.

'Sandy, this is Stella,' said Pandora, laughing, 'she's a librarian. Stella, this is Dr Fanshawe, Sandy for short.'

Dr Fanshawe let go of the girls and gave Stella his hand.

'*Stella Maris*, Star of the Sea, welcome on board the

Amaryllis, Flower of the Sea.'

'Don't mind him,' said a man who was standing behind
Dr Fanshawe, 'he was born in Ireland and we all know
what the Irish are like when they wax lyrical.'

Dr Fanshawe laughed good-humouredly and gave the
man a mock punch in the stomach.

'Come on, girls, I'll show you to your cabins. You can
get into your bikinis.' Briskly he preceded them down the
companion. Stella, who was walking behind him, noticed
that he wore his hair long at the back.

'Stella, you are sharing this cabin with Camilla. She'll
look after you.'

Stella was about to ask where Pandora was going to
sleep (there were only two berths in the cabin) when she
saw Pandora disappearing into another cabin with Dr
Fanshawe. Disappointed, she flopped down on the bottom bunk and looked at Camilla. She hardly knew
Camilla. She had never spent any time with her in the
flat; Camilla was always away. For a moment or two she
stared at this stranger's face, studying its features, trying
to find something familiar about them that would make it
look less strange. A cold, empty feeling that started in the
pit of the stomach gradually crept over her. She did not
know that girl . . . and that girl did not know her. She
watched Camilla unpacking her night bag, taking off her
dress, getting into a swimsuit.

When she was ready, Camilla turned round and seeing
Stella there on the edge of the berth, asked, 'Are you
coming?'

'Where?'

'Up on deck, we're all going for a swim before the
Amaryllis puts out to sea.'

'Puts out to sea!' exclaimed Stella, flabbergasted.

'Yes, what's wrong with that? I'll see you on deck.'

'No, wait. I know it sounds silly but I get sea-sick. Has

Dr Fanshawe got any of those anti-sickness wrist bands? My mother wears them, she says they're effective.'

'No, I don't think so, but there are some pills in the drawer underneath the bunk. Help yourself.'

'Thank you, I will. You've been here before, haven't you?'

'Yes, why?'

'You seem to know the ropes . . . .'

'Dr Fanshawe likes things done in a certain way . . . . I really must go now.'

Stella flopped down on the bunk again. She bent over, opened the drawer and took out the pills. She held them together so tightly in her hand that they began to melt and made her fingers sticky. She got up, looked for a glass of water, swallowed a few pills and washed her hands. Not knowing what to do next, she stood in the middle of the cabin floor, thinking how nice it would be if she could go up on deck with Pandora. Pandora knew all Dr Fanshawe's guests. She had such an easy social manner; she would have made her feel at home; she would have shown her round. Perhaps if she waited long enough, Pandora would come back for her; but first she had to be sure that Pandora was still with Dr Fanshawe. Stella went over to the door, opened it slightly and peered. Dr Fanshawe's own door was shut. Muffled sounds came from inside the cabin. She decided to step outside to listen more closely but, as she did so, she heard Dr Fanshawe's door being unlatched and stepped back inside just in time to bolt the door. Listening behind it, she heard footsteps and suppressed giggles. Then there was a knock on the door. She held her breath and waited, her eyes riveted on the handle. Presently someone outside tried the handle several times. Then a man's voice said quite loudly: 'Camilla! What the f. . . .g hell are you playing at in there? Get your arse up on deck at once and take the well-read asteroid with you!'

Then Stella heard Pandora's voice.

'Lay off, Sandy. She's probably suffering from jet lag.'

Stella waited until the footsteps had died away. Panic-stricken, she rushed out of the cabin and ran up the companion. Dr Fanshawe and Pandora were bound to come across Camilla somewhere on deck and realize it was she who had locked herself in the cabin and was probably still there alone.

Stealthily, Stella made her way aft. Fortunately, most of the guests were busy jumping into the sea from starboard. Pandora and Dr Fanshawe were getting ready to dive in together. Stella ran fore and bumped into Camilla who was tying up her hair.

'Oh there you are! Are you going in?' asked Camilla.

'No, not just yet.'

'Well, don't wait too long!'

Exhausted, Stella sank into a deck chair. She could hear screams down below and laughter, and the silly banter of people fooling about in the water. She wished someone would come and start a conversation with her; it would give her the countenance she lacked, sitting isolated from the rest. One by one the guests were climbing back on board. Stella's sense of alienation became acutely painful. She felt different, defenceless, and all those feelings were an embarrassment to her; she wished the deck would open up and swallow her, thus ridding her of the burden of her self-consciousness.

Pandora emerged like a siren from the sea; she looked stunning in a yellow bikini. She picked up an exotic-looking towel and wrapped it up round her hips. Dr Fanshawe shook the water out of his ears then started to rub himself down. He stood only a few feet away from the spot where Stella was lying down; she had no choice but to observe him. He was middle-aged; he was thick set; he

100

had a hairy chest. Stella averted her face so that he wouldn't see that she had been watching him. She took an instant dislike to the way he was posturing in his bathrobe like an histrionic Roman.

'Ah, the celestial body,' he exclaimed when finally he caught sight of Stella in the deck chair, 'Do you read James Joyce, *Stella Maris*?' "Mary, Star of the Sea", does that mean anything to you?'

Stella squirmed. He was exposing her; he was stripping off her clothes; he was throwing her to the Philistines as a butt.

'*Ulysses*, that's where the expression comes from. Have you read *Ulysses*, Stella Maris?' Dr Fanshawe went on, 'only an Irishman could handle the English language this way. "The voice of prayer to her who is in her pure radiance a beacon to the storm-tossed heart of man, Mary, Star of the Sea." What do you say to that, eh?'

'She's too smart to say anything,' said someone behind Stella. She turned round to see who had spoken. It was the young man who crewed for Dr Fanshawe. He was carrying a pail and started mopping up the water that had dripped off the swimmers on to the deck. 'She'd have to be daft to take anything you say seriously.'

Stella held her breath. The young man had sounded so brash yet so solemn. Dr Fanshawe burst out laughing, did a couple of handstands, picked up his towel and chucked it at Pandora who threw it back at him. Meantime, Camilla had spied the doctor's bath mules lying about on the deck. She collected them, waved the pair at him and in a fit of laughter, slung them overboard. Stella saw her chance. She leapt out of the deck chair and taking advantage of the pandemonium that had broken out on deck, ran back down to the cabin, and climbed into the upper bunk.

She was not alone for long. Shortly after her flight from

the deck the other two joined her. She could hear them rummaging through their beauty cases on the bunk below where they squatted. Camilla said something about Pandora's hair, 'I had better start twining it into braids,' or words to that effect. For a while Stella occupied her mind by trying to follow the drift of the girls' conversation, but it was so disconnected that she could only grasp snips here and there and eventually gave it up. She felt drowsy and ascribed the lethargy which was slowly overcoming her to the sea-sickness pills she had taken earlier on. By and by she became conscious of a lull; things had got very quiet on the *Amaryllis*. She thought of the word 'Twilight' because it described the change in the atmosphere on the yacht very aptly and wondered if it really meant what it had always conveyed to her 'between two lights . . . .'

When she woke up, the *Amaryllis* was moving under engine power – they were sailing and it was dark! She could hear the sound of music up above, now soft, now loud, and the thumping of feet like people dancing. On the cabin floor amongst discarded articles of clothing and lacy underwear she espied a piece of paper. She climbed down to pick it up; it was a note from Pandora saying, 'Don't miss the party.' As she stood on the floor in her bare feet she felt the vibrations of the engine increasing in intensity and intermittently reaching a climax like a shudder; the *Amaryllis* was picking up steam. She poured herself a glass of water; her mouth felt dry after her drug-induced slumber. She thought it would do her good to go up on deck and get some fresh air. She had brought with her a long white dress; it fell in loose folds from a high-waisted bodice; it was a tunic sort of affair in which she felt wonderfully free. To go with it she had purchased a pair of gold sandals with pretty flowers made of coloured beads sewn on the thongs; they too made her feel light and perky. The outfit gave her the sense of a new and exciting identity when she put it on. Delighted with it, she tripped out of the cabin and skipped up the companion. When she emerged in the open air, she found the deck teeming with people. She had no idea that the *Amaryllis* had sailed with so many passengers; there weren't that number of berths on board to accommodate them all. Some of the guests were sitting round the deck; others were lying down on it; a few were dancing. Stella wandered about looking for Dr Fanshawe's young man. She would have liked to engage him in conversation, but when she found him he was standing at the helm and she dared not disturb him. Presently she caught sight of Pandora. She was dancing with a tall, athletic-looking man whose anointed muscles glistened in the single light that flooded the deck. They were both being watched by Dr Fanshawe. He stood on the edge of the dance floor, clapping his hands and stamping his feet to the tune of Ravel's Bolero while his guests gathered in a semi-circle round the dancers. As the tempo increased, so Pandora took off the top she wore over her bikini bra; the young man simultaneously removed a red hair band from his forehead and threw it to one of the guests; then slowly he stripped down to the waist. Pandora untied the *pareo* that was draped round her hips and let it fall to the ground. Dr Fanshawe started cheering and the guests cheered too. Still dancing, Pandora pulled on the red ribbon she wore on the top of her head; a multitude of tiny plaits fell from it. She shook her head several times to loosen the braids then, smiling, she began to take some of them out. Her long fingers caressed the silken hair as she unravelled the snake-like strands to the rhythmic chanting of the spectators. The sight turned Stella to stone . . . she had beheld the Medusa. She stood rooted to the spot, unable to run away. Mesmerised, she watched Pandora take off her bra and toss it in the air. The young man unbuckled the belt which girded his hips and let his trousers drop to the deck. Women screamed and began tearing off their clothes and throwing them at him. Then the spotlight went out. Someone carrying a burning brand came forward from round the back; the flame flickered in the sea breeze as they advanced, carrying it high above the heads of the guests. By the light of its intermittent flares the two dancers finished stripping; when they had done, they turned face to face and, coming slowly forward, met and embraced each other's nakedness. All hell broke loose, or so it seemed to Stella. There were bodies writhing all over the place. Appalled, she decided to pick her way out by high-stepping over them. The sighting of the Gorgon that had frozen her blood earlier on had been cancelled by a much more horrific vision, one that caused flight rather than petrifaction; she was at long last able to move. She was just reaching a clear space in the bows when she collided with Dr Fanshawe's young man. He caught her by the arm to steady her up then, while he held her, he began to stroke her breasts. She could see his eyes staring vacantly into space with hardly a glimmer of recognition in them. She thrust him aside; while he dithered like an inebriated dolt, she ran to the railings, crouched down on to the gunwale and slithered into the sea.

13

The seven coaches came to a halt in Hyde Park. From Knightsbridge to Hyde Park Corner they parked bumper to bumper. Out of the first two came women and children; from the other five, ex-servicemen in uniform alighted. There was a frantic rush for the public conveniences. When everybody had freshened up, they emerged from the underground toilets ready to take in the sights the capital had to offer. Objects of curiosity abounded and continuously claimed their attention in different directions, not least the posse of London Bobbies who stood by the park gates ready to step into line and escort them all the way to Whitehall; the children were fascinated by them. But above all, Hyde Park itself captivated young and old. The trees in the park still had a lot of leaves. The autumnal colours they displayed with many varied shades from the topmost to the lowest branches were carried through on the ground by a motley carpet of leaves spread around the bases of their trunks. Endless vistas of landscaped gardens opened up in the gaps between these enormous trees. As the marchers gazed, bowled over by the amplitude of the scenery that enlivened the heart of the city, they marvelled at the way they felt. They had come up from the country where they were used to big open spaces with woods and rolling fields, yet nothing they had ever seen in their rural environment had affected them in the same way. Faced with the broad, sweeping majesty of the park layout, they felt like yokels. Many of them attributed their susceptibility to the receptive mood they were in; although Major Carrington had warned them against optimism, few of them could deny that they entertained great expectations from their march in the capital. A voice shouting orders broke the spell.

'Come on! Don't stand there gawking,' bellowed Sergeant Bates, 'Action . . . StaSHUN!'

The women rushed to the rear of the coaches and started to pull their placards and posters out of the luggage boots where they had been stacked on leaving Aldershot. The stronger, taller women, who had been assigned the task of displaying the posters, picked them up and hoisted them. The other women had the charge of the children; they lifted the younger ones on to their shoulders and took the older ones by the hand; together they made up the vanguard of the procession. As their group moved off, so a number of policemen fell into line and strode out on its flanks, then came the second group, entirely made up by servicemen in uniform, looking spruce. With pride they filed past, determined to outshine the Bobbies. Their steps on the London pavement rang out with the boldness of seasoned troopers, marching for their lives. Ahead of them went their nearest and dearest, a spearhead thrust into the unknown, on the shift of destiny. Through their own brisk pace, they let their wives and children know they were behind them every inch of the way, ready to back them up – up to the hilt. Not that they doubted their wives' determination; those lasses were staunch supporters of the cause. They had shown their mettle before, on the occasion of the first petition here in London.

The two groups swung round out of the park gates. While they waited for the traffic lights to change, Oliver Carrington disengaged himself from the crowd on the pavement outside Hyde Park Corner tube station and took up his appointed place in the front row of the men's party between his two sergeants; forth he went with them as soon as the traffic lights turned green. An electric feeling ran through the ranks. Smiles broke over the faces of the women who made up the rear of the forward group as they passed down the word – the Major wore manoeuvre dress!

They were drawing level with the Royal Artillery monument, opposite the old hospital, when a child broke away from its mother. Darting in and out of traffic, it made a dash for the monument, clambered up on it and attempted to lift the bronze overcoat from the face of the soldier who lay dead underneath. The mother called it back several times, but her voice was drowned by the roar of the traffic and the child went on straining. In desperation the mother left her place in the procession and went and got the child. The other women slowed down to give her a chance to make it back to the rank across the traffic. Oliver, realizing what had happened, motioned his men to slacken pace; they stamped on the spot for a few minutes and then lurched forward again. Down Constitution Hill, round Queen Victoria's monument, into Spur Road, down Birdcage Walk they went. The women who led the way had been briefed in advance as to the itinerary they were to follow. They did not know London well. The first time they petitioned Whitehall, they travelled up to the capital by rail and just walked the short distance between Waterloo Station and the Government offices in Whitehall.

The march was now passing Wellington Barracks. While going about their business in the yard, the Guards noticed the procession. They stopped attending and watched from behind the railings. The women, when they saw the Guards' eyes on them, slowed down, slightly

107

turned the posters they bore aloft towards the Guards so they could read the slogans. Hoarse hurrahs greeted the placard which spelt out in big black letters 'Heroes overseas, scum at home'. The Guards kept repeating it over and over again with ever-increasing gusto; they said it beat the lot. Oliver, on hearing the commotion in the yard, pressed on; the men who marched with him took their cue from him; they too quickened their steps and passed on without acknowledging the cheers which issued from behind the barracks railings, thus propelling the women forward.

As the demonstrators continued their progress down Birdcage Walk, people in St.James's Park stopped to read the slogans advertising the enlargements of Rebecca Flemington's photographs. 'Save our children from drugs' read the one above the discarded syringes. The posters carried by the tallest women at the rearguard, by their very height, claimed more attention from onlookers than any of the others; they were the ones displaying the swastikas Rebecca Flemington had photographed on the Copeland Estate. The captions coupled with them read 'Save our children from neo-Nazis' and 'Hitler recruits in Farnborough?' Many of the notices were just inscriptions in black paint on white boards, no photographs illustrated them. 'Keep Civvy Street clean' and 'Freedom with morality is what we want' were two examples. On reading those, many of the spectators wondered if the marchers belonged to a religious sect, if they were fundamentalists campaigning for their rights, but once the women's group had gone past and servicemen in uniform came into their view, they realized the military flavour of the militancy made nonsense of their speculation about religious fanaticism. The military party, walking resolutely behind the women who exhibited these extraordinary campaign-cries, emphasized their gist; it gave them the memorability of catch-phrases. In the front row of this martial squad, there walked a tall man in a camouflage suit, who obviously meant business. His assertive bearing, his sprightly step, the eager look on his face arrested attention. He had a big sensual nose; at the top of it, furrows knitted his brows together, giving his face a reflective cast which was daunting to some bystanders. His eyes were magnetic and piercing, but the sharpness all these traits reflected was tempered by the tenderness of his mouth, the corners of which smiled. It was manifest that he commanded respect in his own camp. The men who marched alongside him did so with restraint, in deference to his stature.

It was not until the protest march emerged into Great George Street on its final lap to Whitehall that the television technicians really turned their cameras on it. Up to then the march had been photographed here and there by newspaper men. The BBC Outside Broadcast vehicle had appeared and disappeared at various stage points, but no real confrontation with the media had taken place. Oliver had not the slightest intention of being inveigled by any of them. This was a serious business. He was not prepared to let those glib cavaliers of the Here and Now turn it into an ephemera of no moment – too much levity had already demeaned the cause. There were women and children involved in this rally; they had left their homes at crack of dawn. One only had to look at them to feel compassion for them. Many were tired and hungry. The women who carried the posters had cramps in their arms; some of the shanks were rough and blistered their fingers . . . .

The women's group came to a halt in Whitehall. Outside the Government offices a crowd quickly gathered round the demonstrators, who were immediately surrounded by police. In Whitehall people got off buses and ran across the traffic to try and break through the cordon; more came from Parliament Square and over Westminster Bridge. They wore labels on their coats with Hong Kong and Gibraltar written across them. They said that they had heard about the protest march through the grapevine and were anxious to give their support to the movement. Children were getting jostled by these enthusiastic newcomers as they shoved to join their comrades inside the ring made by the police; many mothers had a hard time protecting their offspring from them. To add to the mayhem, the BBC Outside Broadcast crew, the television cameramen and the newspaper reporters all converged on the scene at the same time. Oliver became anxious for the children's safety; he feared that they would get crushed if he did not interfere. He lifted up his arms and asked the late-comers to desist from any further hustle.

'Not that your spontaneous gesture of solidarity is not appreciated,' he told them, 'the more protesters there are, the quicker this Government will realize soldiers are not to be trifled with. But this being a peaceful demonstration, run within the confines of the law, it is imperative everybody connected with it should hold their peace for the benefit of all concerned.'

'That's all right for you, governor,' one of the manifestants shouted when Oliver stopped speaking, 'you've probably got a house of your own, but my wife, my kids and myself, we're rotting away in a bed and breakfast without cooking facilities. So don't you lecture me about holding my peace. I don't give a shit for peace, it stinks.'

A battery of cameras turned instantly on Oliver; journalists and reporters rushed up to him with microphones, mindless of the children who stood in the way. They began shooting questions at him.

'Sir . . . Sir . . . would you say that parading swastikas is not endangering public peace?'

'Sir, exhibiting swastikas is a provocation to incendiaries, yet you talk of peace . . . .'

'Sir, you advocate "Freedom with morality". Would you disagree with the view that complete freedom should comprise immorality as well as morality?'

'These are leading questions, tendencious questions wrested from our central message,' replied Oliver. 'I am not prepared to comment. I am here on an errand, not a quiz. My errand here is to obtain good homes for these good people.'

At that point, a spokesman from the Ministry of Defence appeared gingerly in a doorway. In a trice all the pressmen, cameramen and newsmen wheeled away from Oliver and concentrated their fire on the Minister's envoy. Scores of microphones were thrust at him. Speaking into the nearest one, the spokesman said that the Minister and his staff had been aware of the difficulties of the resettlement problem and every effort had been made to overcome them in the best possible way.

'Go home,' was all he could tell them. 'Your requirements have been noted, but one thing I must make clear to you: the resettlement of hundreds of thousands of redundant soldiers in the UK does not allow for them to be catered for individually,' and he concluded by wishing them 'God speed'.

'You bloody bastard!' someone in the ranks shouted as the Minister's spokesman made a hurried exit. Boos and jeers from Oliver's party greeted the insult. Any antisocial behaviour which was damaging to the cause had to be decried right away.

Oliver had a quick word with his sergeants. Before they could even think about marching back to the coaches in Hyde Park, they had to get rid of the last-minute supporters; their intentions were suspect, Oliver feared.

'How are we going to lose them, Sir?' asked Sergeant Bates. 'There are trouble-makers among them.'

No sooner had Sergeant Bates finished speaking than one of the malcontents began to swear at the constable who was urging him to move along, so that the procession could get under way. Others followed suit. When they realized shouting abuse was not going to get them anywhere, they threw themselves on the ground, intent on obstructing.

Oliver, who was at the ready, surrounded himself with a few henchmen and stepped forward.

'Let me deal with this, Constable. After all, I am in charge of this march. I'll speak to those desperados.'

The Constable agreed. He told his colleagues, who were about to grasp the obstructionists by the arms and drag them away, to stop.

When he saw Oliver and his sergeants striding over to where they lay, one of the dissidents shouted, 'Come on, you two-faced baboons! Aren't you going to roll up your sleeves and slog the grunters? Gone soft, have you? Too much nookie on Saturday night in the disco, eh?'

Oliver bent down, picked the chap up by the collar of his denim jacket and set him on his feet with a vicious thump. 'All right! all right, Governor! No need to get hot under the collar. I was only trying to help.'

'One of these days, your filthy temper will get you into trouble, soldier, unless you do something about it,' whispered Oliver right up close to the chap's ear. While he spoke under his breath he deftly slipped a card in his top pocket; then he let go of him and, in a loud voice, for all to hear, said, 'Dismiss!'

The offender faltered forward, straightening up his clothes; while beating his chest to shake the dust out of his jacket, he felt the card Oliver had placed in one of the breast pockets. A grin broke over his face. He smoothed down his tousled hair, then touching his forehead in a mock military salute sauntered away to the spot where his mates were squatting.

'Get up,' he said, 'and follow me.'

*   *   *

Rebecca wondered what was keeping the marchers from returning to Hyde Park on time; they were at least one hour behind schedule. Anxiously she reviewed all the possible causes of delay – scuffles with militant factions, clashes with the police, encounters with gangs of hooligans on the rampage or quite simply the London traffic. Before leaving Aldershot, she had spent hours packing foodstuff into hampers and cool boxes. She had filled her car to capacity with provisions. She had catered for children, she had catered for adults; for women with a sweet tooth, for men with a preference for savouries. For Oliver she had prepared very special fare with lots of mustard and relish – pickles, chili sauce, Worcester sauce, horseradish sauce, chutney, piccalilli, anchovy paste – smoked salmon, thin-sliced brown bread and butter, crisp cheese crackers, his favourite Stilton fortified with vintage Port, and even a dozen oysters packed on crushed ice with crimped slices of lemon.

She had parked her car behind the coaches so as to be able to use the boot as a buffet. She would have liked to stretch her legs in the park, but the thought of the hungry marchers kept her right by the food. Also she had promised the wives she would photograph them with their posters as soon as they returned. As time went by and there were still no signs of the party, she felt more and more tempted to leave her car and go for a stroll in Hyde Park. Its beauty beckoned her. From where she stood she could see an abundance of views that appealed to her

113

aesthetic sense. She had so few opportunities for landscape photographs . . . .

But there they were, coming back! In small groups, with stragglers of all ages, they looked weary. She rushed to meet them, waving her camera in the air.

'Come on, buck up! I can't photograph you with long faces. Come on, cheer up! Say "cheese" and smile, smile, smile!'

One of the women recognised her.

'Miss Flemington! Thank God, you've come! We were held up in Whitehall. There was a hustle with outsiders.'

'Oh, dear! Well, was the march a success? Was the Press there?'

'Oh, yes, they were there all right, and the television cameras and the BBC.'

'Oh, good. Major Carrington was pleased then?'

'He was! He gave the reporters a piece of his mind.'

'By the way, where is he now?' asked Rebecca, looking round. 'Where is the Major?'

'Oh, he's gone!'

'What do you mean, gone?'

'Gone back. He left my husband and the other men to get his car out of the multi-storey car park in Park Lane. He told them he had some urgent business to attend to in Aldershot.'

Rebecca's heart sank, 'The brute,' she thought, 'the beastly brute!' The invective welled up spontaneously, upsetting her by its fierceness. She kept repeating it, over and over again, as if to placate her bitter disappointment. She was not duped – the urgent business Carrington had to attend to in Aldershot could only be Stella. Nothing else would have lured him away from the march and its people on such an important day.

14

'Miss Flemington is here, Sir.'

'All right, let her in, Morton. Rebecca, my dear, how nice of you to call on an old campaigner! And how is life treating you these days?'

'Please spare me the prattle, Wallace, I've come to say goodbye.'

'Dear me, that sounds drastic. You emigrating or something?'

'No, Wallace, I am not going anywhere. I shan't see you any more, that is all.'

'Oh,' uttered the Colonel, taken aback by Rebecca's declaration.

'Don't bother to send me any more birthday or Christmas cards. Don't write to me for the anniversary of Flemmie's death.'

Colonel Wallace stared at his visitor with bewilderment. 'I don't think I understand, Rebecca.'

'Oh, yes, you do! You understand perfectly well what I mean. All those years when you could have given me love, you chose to play the avuncular part because it fitted a stereotype which was accepted in the conventional circles in which you moved. You never showed me any real signs of affection. You never loved me.'

'Why didn't you say?' whispered Colonel Wallace, aghast.

115

'Say!' exclaimed Rebecca. 'What can an independent, sexually-mature girl say to an older man that is not likely to be misconstrued?'

'What on earth has brought all this about, Rebecca? You're unreasonable!'

'Go on, say it! It's on the tip of your tongue, "like your mother".'

Colonel Wallace nodded his head.

'Your mother couldn't have had a more devoted husband. Flemmie worshipped the ground she trod on. But it wasn't enough.'

'I'm not going to listen to this!' Rebecca picked up her shoulder bag and made for the door.

'Come to the club on Sunday!' Colonel Wallace shouted as she brushed past Morton.

'I'm going to be too busy for Sunday luncheons,' she retorted.

'Rebecca!' the Colonel called after her, but it was too late, she had gone out of the front door, ahead of the batman.

The Colonel stood there shaking. Who would have thought such a scene possible between two people who had known each other for so long? Rebecca was such a charming girl; she had such nice manners, and underneath it all there brewed this vile ferment of bitterness and resentment. God only knew how long it had been there! He had entertained such high hopes for her. Only recently he had introduced her to Oliver Carrington, thinking what a splendid companion she would make for him during the difficult transition period between Army and civilian life, but it didn't look as though things had turned out quite as he expected. Both these young people gave the impression of having reached a crisis in their lives. Redundancy had triggered off the crisis in Oliver's life, but Rebecca's, what had brought that about? Evidently

116

she had harboured a grievance against her father's oldest friend for years, but nothing until now had caused this rancour to erupt, and it wasn't a mild eruption, far from it. It had brought up such pent-up bitterness, such deep-seated resentment, such ill-temper, it must have been latent for a considerably long time. Did Oliver have anything to do with it? He might have precipitated the crisis in Rebecca's life by behaving in a way that upset her emotional balance. Only something to do with the affairs of the heart could have provoked Rebecca's phrenetic outburst 'You never loved me!' The meaning of that cry, coming straight from the heart, did not elude him; he understood its message very well although he was an old man out of touch with women. It said, 'had you loved me, I would not be so unhappy now'.

Be that as it may, the crisis in both these young persons' lives had had the same disastrous effect – it had clouded their judgment. Both of them were in a state of rebellion when they might do silly things just for the sheer hell of it. It was such a pity! Both possessed outstanding qualities which made them special people. It would be tragic if they were to lead each other astray and waste their talents on madcap schemes, instead of pursuing normal lives.

*   *   *

Colonel Wallace let the newspaper drop on his lap. The news was terrible, a real disaster. It confirmed his worst fears about Oliver. Gloom enveloped him; he felt himself shrinking inwardly with shame and all of a sudden he was aware for the first time that he was old, very old. No matter what newspaper he picked up, the headlines all said more or less the same thing:

'Rabble-rousing Major goes to town'

'Ex-tank officer leads his band of Tommy Dissenters'

117

'Redundant Army officer raises standard of Puritan rebellion'

'Old Roundhead battle-cry sounds again'

The night before on television, much to his chagrin, he had seen Oliver engaged in a battle of wits with the media, right on the doorstep of the Ministry of Defence, a compromising situation if ever there was one for an officer, even a redundant one. In any case, there was no such thing as a redundant officer – once an officer, always an officer. The status was not a transitory one. Oliver would die an officer. In Whitehall, he had publicly declared himself the champion of those nincompoops; he had publicly burnt his bridges. What for? In the name of what? It was incomprehensible. Why put oneself in that insidious position? Why not leave well alone? Why not accept once and for all the imperfections of an imperfect world? Were those goody-goodies worth making such a song and dance about? During the death-throes of empires, history had always claimed hapless victims, often in a gory way. Those silly blighters should have counted themselves lucky their rise and fall had not been brought about by a public calamity, just a gentle withdrawal of troops. What was all the blather about?

He had always looked on Oliver as his son, the son he had never had. Since last night, he could no longer think of him in a paternal way without being afflicted by an acute sense of betrayal. Not that loyalty had weighed for much when Oliver came to make his choice. As for Rebecca, her disloyalty was perhaps greater than Oliver's. She had been thoroughly deceitful. She had concealed from him her real feelings, year in, year out. Outwardly charming, yet seething with animosity. It was a terrible thought, more terrible even than the thought he had been instrumental in bringing those two together. Thank God her father was dead! He didn't have to shatter

118

his old friend's illusions about his daughter's character.

Although he could not adduce any evidence, his conviction grew that Oliver and Rebecca were in league (he might be feeling old, but his brain was not addled). They were a couple of vagabonds, engaged in seditious ventures. In spite of their having inflicted pain on him, his heart bled for them, but he could not allow his personal feelings to interfere with the line it was his duty to take.

15

Rebecca hurried through St James's Park. She knew she was late in keeping her appointment with Oliver; she had been unable to find a parking space for her car conveniently near the park, an aggravation she did not need at this stage. She felt flustered enough at the thought of meeting Oliver. He had summoned her! She did so want to appear relaxed and carefree, in spite of having a guilty conscience.

She had not seen him since the day of the protest march, when he had left them all 'in the lurch', or so she thought rashly at the time. She had reacted strongly to his default and the memory of it still rankled. She was cross with herself on two counts – first for having over-reacted, secondly for having taken for granted that he would be available at the end of the march, thus prepossessing his freedom, and of the two she felt more ashamed of the latter. As she sped along down the park's alleyways, she caught sight of Oliver standing in the middle of the bridge. He was leaning over the rail and appeared to be staring at the water, deep in thought. She really did not know what to anticipate; he smiled when he saw her.

'Shall we walk?' he asked.

'Why not?' she replied. (She had already gone right round the park to find the bridge; a few more hundred yards would not make all that much difference) 'So long as we stay close to the water!'

'Close to the water? Why the proviso?'

'Ducks! I love ducks.'

'You know what the Chinese say about them?'

'They're symbolic of connubial bliss . . . . No, it's their shapes I find irresistibly attractive. I could photograph them all day long.'

He ambled along, looking round, as though he didn't have a care in the world. Nonchalant, when she herself was agog with curiosity . . . .

'I watched the nine o'clock news the day of the march . . . .' She thought she had better broach the subject since he seemed keen to keep his counsel 'I thought you did pretty well on the whole.'

'Yes, we did, didn't we?'

'I mean, it could lead to bigger things . . . .'

He shook his head pensively and stared at the ground as he strolled along.

'Yes, indeed. Things could come to a head. Public opinion has changed, as I know from all the letters I receive. I hadn't realised to what extent it had changed. The response from people in all walks of life has been incredible.'

'And the Army?'

'It depends what you mean by the Army. If you mean the Top Brass Brigade, they won't budge. I pin all my hopes on the young and on the TA volunteers.'

'The Reservists! What makes you say that?'

'They're taught to bloody well shoot straight!' Oliver replied, and having said this he burst out laughing. 'No, what I meant was, a lot of them are under the threat of redundancy as civilians.'

By then they had come full circle and were back on the bridge. She stopped and leant over the railing to look at the ducks.

'What will you do?' she asked softly.

121

'I'm not sure. A rally in Trafalgar Square is a possibility to test the masses. We need the support of the masses now.'

'Some say they're the true makers of history . . . .'

'If one could shake their complacent habits of self-deception and servile deference to the aristocracy. The moral and intellectual fibre of the country has been weakened by those habits. They have brought the country to a state of social and cultural degeneracy. None of the cliches that make us tick bear critical examination; they all sound hollow after scrutiny. It would take a revolution to bring about regeneration.'

'Is there is anything I can do to help?' she hazarded.

'I believe you've become popular with the men's wives,' he replied looking at her with a kindly smile.

'You mean, I gave them sandwiches after the march. By the way, how is Stella?' It was daring of her to ask, but if she had to take the plunge, she might as well do it headlong at the right conjunction.

'Stella? Oh yes, she had an accident.'

'What, riding?'

'No, swimming. She nearly drowned, off Cowes.'

'What on earth was she doing in Cowes?'

'Yachting. Isn't that what people do in Cowes?' he asked with a twinkle in his eyes. 'She'd gone with Pandora and lot of other debauchees to a party on a yacht.'

'Oh . . . . Didn't they have lifebelts on board?'

'Yes, they did, but you don't go round looking for lifebelts when you're trying to escape from the unwelcome advances of a male, do you?'

'No, not unless you want to get laid! And where is the "blameless vestal" now? On the south-east side of the Forum?'

'You know, that last remark of yours could sound quite funny, if it were in a different context.'

'Meaning "we are not amused"? Right?'
'Right.'
'So, presumably Stella is not going back to Pandora's?'
'No, it wasn't congenial. She is staying with me at the Masseys' in Aldershot. She is still shaken.'

*   *   *

The announcement galvanized Rebecca. Whereas, earlier on, it might have upset her, the progress she had been making in introspective therapy enabled her to receive it in a constructive way. The minute Oliver broke the news to her, the system she had devised for sorting out her emotions came into play; all irrelevancies fell away and she was able to register the one central piece of intelligence. Erasing all other extraneous data, it scored a triumph in subjective economy. She had become a deft hand at using the system. The untidy stage she had gone through emotionally just before the protest march had sickened her; she never wanted to go through anything as depressing as that again.

The thought of Stella's physical weakness, her personal disasters and resultant traumas had a tonic effect on her. What debilitated Stella, when she reviewed it, invigorated her, and the fact that Stella now lived under the same roof as Oliver faded into insignificance when weighed against this very gainful boost.

Now that she had jettisoned her father's old friend, thereby casting off the shackles of the past and the accoutrements thereof, she felt free to forge ahead as a new woman. It mattered little to her that the traumas Stella suffered were perhaps linked to Stella's temperamental frailty – someone of a less impressionable disposition might have reacted differently and suffered to a lesser degree – the injuries Stella sustained became grounds for general concern and a source of militant inspiration.

Moral principles were extracted from Stella's misfortunes. Rebecca viewed these principles with the same sharpness of vision with which as a photographer she looked at natural objects. To give them good definition, she brought them into hard focus, but in the process Stella, the private individual, vanished. By a piece of psychological sleight she was lost sight of. She dissolved into thin air and passed into the Kingdom of Shades, depersonalized; only her wounds remained on view in the foreground as pre-eminent exhibits, abstracted from her and magnified beyond identification by dint of legerdemain. The spectacle of those traumatic objects Rebecca found offensive; it generated in her an irresistible impulse towards radical solutions to the problems of evil. She found herself moving fast in the direction of very advanced positions, both ethical and political, and the views that she embraced on the way to those far-flung outposts of rectitude, frightened her by their audacity. She kept telling herself that all she needed was extra courage in order to imbibe those radically novel views and accept them calmly as her very own. Once she had mustered that additional fortitude, then she could perform her rites of passage. Only through the performance of those rites could she gain access to the higher sphere where Oliver functioned. That he had been a life-long tenant of a secure moral habitat was plain; everything about him proclaimed it; he was essentially a just man, and what she hankered after most was to join him on home ground.

INTERLUDE

News from the South

'An attack of unprecedented violence took place last night on the yacht *Amaryllis* as she lay at anchor in her mooring at Cowes. Extensive damage was done to the engine-room but the vandals seem to have concentrated their fury on the cabins where they created havoc. The yacht belonged to Dr Fanshawe, a consultant from the mainland, a regular weekend visitor to the island. Dr Wells, one of Dr Fanshawe's partners, was interviewed in Portsmouth a few hours after the discovery of the attack. Dr Wells said, "Dr Fanshawe is a respected member of the community. I can't think who would want to commit such an outrage except some kind of maniac. Dr Fanshawe has over the years treated a number of mentally disturbed patients and junkies. In view of the fact that large quantities of pills were found below deck in the yacht's toilets, the surmise here in the practice is that we may be dealing with an act of violence committed by an ex-patient to whom Dr Fanshawe may have refused access to further supplies of drugs".'

'Are you saying then, Dr Wells, that the motive behind the havoc on the *Amaryllis* was resentment leading to revenge?'

'This would be in line with the current medical view of the actions of a particular type of psychopath.'

'Thank you, Dr Wells.'

Meanwhile at Police Headquarters in Portsmouth.

'Found anything?'

'Yes, Sir, this.'

The sergeant took a piece of paper out of his pocket and handed it over to Inspector Smithers, who read out aloud 'Rebecca 1843'.

'What do you make of that then, Matthews?'

'Rebecca's a girl's name, Sir!'

'Thank you, Matthews! But it's the date that bothers me, 1843, that's over a hundred and fifty years ago. Where did you find this piece of paper?'

'Nailed to the steering wheel, Sir.'

'The helm, Matthews, the helm!'

'Sorry, Sir. I'm afraid sailing is not up my street. I only have to look at a boat to feel sick.'

Both men kept silent for a while.

'I've been thinking, Sir . . . .'

The furrows above the inspector's brows deepened. That's what came from increasing the pay! You got the type into the Force that thought their business was to think.

'Let's have it, Matthews.'

'Well, Sir, if you count the letters in Rebecca, there are seven of them and if you add 1843, one plus eight makes nine, plus four makes thirteen plus three makes sixteen, six plus one makes seven. Both clues spell out seven . . . .'

'So?'

'Well, Sir, maybe this is the first of a series of seven disturbances.'

'What we need, Matthews, is a historian, not a crystal-gazer. Only a historian can tell us who Rebecca was and what she was up to in 1843. This means deferring to superior authority in Oxford. Chief Constable Davenport, I believe, is not disinclined to dropping hints about his connections with the universities.'

The telephone bell interrupted the Inspector.

'Smithers, yes, well, what are they?' A shadow fell

126

across the Inspector's face.

'Are you sure? Positive? I see, thanks. Send me the test sheets, will you. It's going to take a lot of written evidence to convince the superintendent this is not an open and shut case.' The Inspector cast a glum look at Sergeant Matthews.

'Those pills they found stuffed down the toilets on board the *Amaryllis*, they were birth-control pills. Forensic are positive. That destroys the junkie presumption.'

'Rebecca!' exclaimed Sergeant Matthews. 'She must have been against birth control!'

'What, in 1843? When did you last have a holiday, Matthews?'

'The wife's just had twins, Sir. Things are a bit tight at the moment.'

Inspector Smithers scowled; he allowed his displeasure to influence his thoughts on the fertility rate of police sergeants.

'What about that painter chap, the one who's come forwards. Have we got his statement yet?'

'Les Gamble, Sir? Oh, yes . . . .'

'Well, what are we waiting for? Let's hear it, now!'

The Painter's Tale, as recorded by the Police on tape

'I'm a freelance painter now, but prior to the attack on the *Amaryllis* I was working for a firm of painters and decorators. The firm did some work for Dr Fanshawe at his house and I happened to be on the team. One day, just before we completed the job, Dr Fanshawe came up to me. He said he'd been watching me and had found me to be the most hard-working and the most thorough of all the chaps on the team. He said he had a yacht at Cowes which needed a coat of paint and he wanted to give me the job, weekends when he was down there; he would make it worth my while. Well, I had never been to Cowes and the idea of spending a few weekends down there did not displease me. The wife's mother wasn't well; the wife was going away every Saturday to look after the old lady, so I was on my own a great deal.

'The first Saturday I went down to Cowes, Dr Fanshawe had me met on the quay by a youngish chap, who, I discovered later, always accompanied him on his week-end trips. As I got into the dinghy, I noticed a girl carrying a holdall standing on the quay. Dr Fanshawe's chap waved to her and said he would come back for her later. Dr Fanshawe was on deck when I stepped aboard. I'm not a prudish man, not by any means, but he did something then that surprised me. He undid his fly and peed over the side into the sea, long and hard in front of me. I couldn't help looking down, I mean, he was an educated man, of the kind one looks up to. "Welcome on board, Les," he said as though nothing had happened.'

" 'Afternoon, Dr Fanshawe," I replied not quite knowing how to handle it. Anyway, to cut a long story short, he showed me what needed doing. The chap who crewed for him had laid up stores and I set to. Now and then, when I needed a break, I'd pull out the flask the wife had got ready for me and had a cuppa and a few puffs of the old fag and prowled around for a minute or two – not that I wanted to be a Nosey Parker, but just to find out how the other half lives, and what the boat was like. She was a nice boat, I'd say that for her, not that I know much about boats. Dr Fanshawe had told me the type of craft she was, but it meant nothing to me. To each his own, I say and if Dr Fanshawe was proud of her. then that was OK by me.'

'You know how it is when you're painting, you lose count of the hours. Suddenly, I noticed a change in the light, the sun was going down. I started to put away my brushes when I heard a noise on the other side of the deck. It sounded like oars striking the water. I heard voices as well and laughter. I peered round the corner to see what was going on. The young chap who had rowed me out to the *Amaryllis* was standing up in the dinghy, helping three girls to alight. My God, they were beautiful and young too, real pin-ups. Dr Fanshawe was standing at the top of the gangway in bathing trunks. I felt trapped. Dr Fanshawe had booked bed and breakfast for me in Cowes and I thought if I could make a bee-line for the gangway as soon as the girls had touched deck, I could get the young man to row me ashore right away. But no such luck, 'cos no sooner had the girls got aboard than a motor launch circled up to the gangway and a whole load of people got off it and started climbing up the side. I was still wearing my white dungarees and felt a right idiot. "Les," Dr Fanshawe said, "Les, meet my guests. This is Pandora. Pandora, come and say hello to Les". I immediately recognized the girl I had seen on the quay earlier on in the day. She was even more beautiful from close up than she had been from a distance. Dr Fanshawe put his arm round her shoulders and bent down to whisper something in her ear. She smiled and said she'd think about it. "Promise?" asked Dr Fanshawe, but she didn't reply, just tossed her head back and shook her beautiful blonde locks, then she freed herself from Dr Fanshawe's embrace and disappeared down the cabin stairs.'

Inspector Smithers switched off the tape.

'What's the painter's name again?' he asked.

'Les Gamble, Sir. What do you think about the tape?'

'Gamble's probably the world's greatest rapist.' The Inspector put away the tape and leant back in his chair. 'Do you remember the raid on the bank at Windsor? The extraordinary thing about that was that no money was stolen from the bank. The charred remains of hundreds of credit cards lay on the floor behind the tills. It looked as though someone had deliberately gathered them into a pile and incinerated them. On the pavement outside the bank, painted in white capitals, was the name "Rebecca" and the date "1839". It was the first time we'd come across the signature and we passed it by; it meant nothing to us . . . .'

Sergeant Matthews nodded and kept silent.

'Do you know what the most powerful motive is, Matthews?' Inspector Smithers asked, looking straight at his sergeant.

'Greed, Sir?' hazarded Matthews.

'No! Revenge. Do you know why?'

'Presumably . . . .'

'Greed does not keep. Revenge does – for years and is all the more compelling for it.'

'Do you think . . . ?'

'Yes! Rebecca, whoever she might be, is an avenger. Look at the dates. 1843, we had the havoc on the *Amaryllis*. 1839, the raid on the bank. That's over three years, Matthews. She is trying to tell us something.'

'As you said, Sir, revenge keeps. But why those old dates in the 21st century? Rebecca can't be a spook.'

'No, but her spirit may be inspiring someone.'

Sergeant Matthews stared at the floor.

'You mean someone contemporary. Sir?'

'Yes, Matthews. someone whose name is also Rebecca, unless, of course, Rebecca is a code name, like the Scarlet Pimpernel or the Jackal. Surely you've heard of them?'

'Yes, Sir, I mean, no, Sir. I don't go in for that sort of fiction.'

Sergeant Matthews waited for a reaction from the Inspector, whose acerbic remarks he had come to expect. When none came, he thought he ought to remind him about the unfinished business.

'About the painter's testimony, Sir, you know the tape we've just listened to . . . ?'

130

'Well, what about it?'

'There's a bit more to come. We haven't heard it all.'

'You mean, I digressed. Digression, Matthews, is the mother of solution. It's the only way to solve a case. It is by getting away from the evidence that one gets close to what really happened.'

'If you say so, Sir. I would have said it was rather unorthodox myself.'

'Yes, Matthews, unorthodox but fruitful. Go on, then, put the blooming tape on.'

'Yes, Sir. Here it comes.'

'Well, eventually Dr Fanshawe's young man did row me ashore and I got to the B and B place and very nice it was. Next morning I'm on the quay waiting to be picked up for the second day and what do I see? I see a female with long wet hair in a white dress trying to climb up on the quay. She keeps trying and each time she falls back exhausted in to the water. Eventually she stops trying and all I can see is a hand clinging to the wall. I pelted down the quayside, grabbed the girl's hand and pulled her clean out of the water. Holy mackerel, I exclaimed! She was one of Dr Fanshawe's guests. I just could not believe my eyes. She had swallowed a lot of water and looked in a bad way. I dragged her to the nearest bollard and made her sit up. She opened her eyes several times and then passed out. I picked her up and started carrying her up and down the quayside not knowing what to do. When she came round, she asked me if I would make a telephone call for her, which I did; it was to a major in Aldershot; I've forgotten his name. I had to tell him Stella had met with an accident, would he come and pick her up. She asked me not to tell anyone about the phone call, she said she knew who I was and where I was going. I didn't feel too happy about leaving her stranded, she was shivering and she looked very pale, but I could see the boat that was picking

131

me up get closer and closer and I had to go. I knew she was being picked up, so I didn't feel too bad about it in the end.'

'That's it, Sir. That's the end of the statement,' said Sergeant Matthews, switching off the tape. 'What do you think?'

'I think he's been watching *King Kong* a little too often.'

'You don't find him credible. then, Sir?'

'Oh, yes, as far as the sexual fantasy goes, I find him very credible. The trouble with you, Matthews, is you are credulous.'

'You don't think she could be Rebecca?'

'Who? The castaway?'

'Yes, bearing in mind what you said earlier on about revenge being a powerful motive, somebody might have tried to kill her on board the *Amaryllis*, or she might have jumped overboard to escape from a sex maniac. Who knows what goes on on board those posh yachts . . . ?'

'If Les Gamble's statement is anything to go by she's much too nice to be Rebecca. Besides, he says her name is Stella. It could have been an accident; these things happen; people do fall overboard.'

Sergeant Matthews reporting to Inspector Smithers several months later, outside Darley Hall:

'At the entrance of the property, at the top of the drive, about two miles away from the blaze, swinging from the branch of a tree, was a black box like the one that is recovered from an aircraft after a crash. The Fire Brigade hadn't noticed it as they hurtled through the gateway on their way to the fire . . . .'

'Go on,' said Inspector Smithers impatiently. 'I do object to this habit you have of beating about the bush.

Why can't you just get on with it?'

'I'm getting round to it, Sir. Well, it was just beginning to get light as we drove through the pillars where once the gate had hung, and there dangling overhead was this black box. I ordered the constable to stop.'

'Why?'

'I don't know, Sir. It seemed odd. For a minute I wondered if a plane had crashed on Darley Hall and caused the fire and that was its black box. Anyway, the constable, who was taller than me, pulled down the branch to be able to reach for the box. As I was wearing gloves I thought I had better grab the box myself. I opened it right away, thinking it contained valuable information about the crash. Inside it was a single sheet of paper, ruled and margin, like a student's notebook, with the word "Rebecca" and another date.'

'Go on!' shouted Inspector Smithers.

' "1842", Sir. Forensic have it, I mean the box.'

'What, with the note?'

'I'm afraid so, Sir. But it was identical to the others, the print, the size of the capitals, the figures, everything tallied.'

'So now we're dealing with an incendiary as well as an avenger,' groaned Inspector Smithers.

The siren of a fire-engine drawing near made the two men jump to one side.

'They're rushing reinforcement from neighbouring divisions, Sir. The local force can't cope, the fire is that wicked, a real pro's job.'

'Come on, Matthews, don't just stand there talking. Move it!'

'Where to, Sir?'

'To the house, Matthews, to the house, for Christ's sake!'

'There's nothing left standing, Sir. Nowhere. The staff

bungalows, the chapel, the gym, the stables, all the outbuildings, everything was ablaze when we arrived. It would seem that the outbuildings were set alight first, obviously by someone who knew the place well. A strong south-westerly swept the flames forwards towards the big house. There was nothing the firemen could do to stop the fire from spreading. In no time at all they were caught between two blazing seats, one of which threatened to cut off their rear.'

Inspector Smithers slumped into the passenger seat of Sergeant Matthews' car. It was unbearable, this flux of words pouring out of his assistant at such a time, as though the fire excited the sergeant, took the lid off all his inhibitions, released a kind of supernatural loquacity and conferred upon him a voluble ego which normally his subordinate position thwarted.

'Is that all?' asked Inspector Smithers, meaning to bring back to reality this unabashed, unbridled young man.

'Yes, Sir, well, no, Sir, not quite,' replied Sergeant Matthews, feeling suddenly deflated.

'What now?'

'Well you see, Sir, on the back of the note, you know with Rebecca and the date, was an inscription. I made a note of it. Ah, here we are, "Genesis XXIV. v. 60".'

'Genesis . . . the first book of Moses . . . .' said Inspector Smithers. 'Well, well, well . . . you're not a Bible reader, are you, Matthews?'

'No. Sir, I'm afraid not.'

'I didn't think you were. Pity, it's very instructive. My father kept the Authorized Version by his bedside. I benefited from it. Come on, let's go!'

As they got out of the car, both men were immediately shrouded in swirls of dust and ashes. Although they stood at a safe distance from the multi-headed monster that rampaged brutally about, they felt intense heat round their heads and at times had to avert their faces from the furnace that generated it with such fierceness. The acute discomfort they felt, however, was to a large extent cancelled by the fascination the fire exerted on them. Its pyrotechnic skill mesmerised them both. It was a spectacle on a grand scale, in the patrician manner, worthy of the house that staged it, such as probably they would never see again. As columns of incandescent material crumbled, so jets sprang up like volcanic geysers and in turn fell back to earth, multiplying uncanny devices, effects of aerial grace and lightness, ephemeral yet continuous, surpassing in beauty anything the human hand could command in that line of entertainment. Flames fluttered and died on beds of embers overhung by intricate chambers with glowing cavities, the activeness of which fascinated both men, and then there was the orchestral music of the conflagration, variations on a fiery theme which never for a minute spared their ears, pricked to a supreme and exhausting degree of attention. Mighty clatters, like cymbals and percussion run amok in the background, would suddenly shatter the symphonic texture of the sound produced by the steady roar of the fire, rousing the spectators to a flaying perception of the disaster.

'Rebecca, the supreme artificer,' muttered Inspector Smithers.

'What's that, Sir?' enquired Sergeant Matthews.

'Oh, nothing, Matthews. Let's go and look for the divisional officer. There must be one about in an inferno of this magnitude,' replied Inspector Smithers, tearing himself away from the entrancing sight.

*   *   *

Several weeks later, after the outrage on the *Amaryllis*,

the raid on the bank at Windsor and the fire that destroyed Darley Hall, Inspector Smithers was in conversation with his sergeant and the other men on his team.

'Chief Constable Davenport of Oxfordshire Constabulary has spoken to a Doctor in History and he has come up with some interesting facts. Rebecca was a gate-breaker in the nineteenth century, the leader of an anti-turnpike conspiracy in Wales; she was a redresser, if you like. She went about doing justice, reforming things that were out of the way. She also handed out punishment to the promiscuous, the sexually deviant, adulterers, wife-beaters and family tyrants. It's an impressive range of activities and I hope our Rebecca is not going to present us with too many punitive expeditions. Matthews?'

'Yes, Sir?'

'Do you remember that inscription on the back of the note Rebecca left in the black box outside Darley Hall?'

'From the Bible, Sir?'

'Yes', Inspector Smithers replied with a far-away look on his face, 'Genesis Chapter twenty-four verse sixty. That particular verse refers to the biblical Rebekah, the one that stood at the well with a pitcher on her shoulder and gave Isaac a drink and watered his camels. When I was a boy, I used to think that was the most romantic meeting in the world. I used to get really worked up about it. I would picture myself as Isaac putting ear-rings on Rebekah's face and bracelets on her hands, by the well, under a palm tree, with camels all around; it was all so exotic and she a virgin, Matthews, and how many of those are there around today, standing by a well, offering drinks?' Inspector Smithers sadly shook his head. 'Not many, Matthews, not many!'

Sergeant Matthews looked down and stared at the floor.

'No, Sir'.

'Now,' Inspector Smithers went on, 'what verse sixty also says about Rebekah is this: 'Be thou the mother of thousands of millions and let thy seed possess the gate of those which hate them'. I find this particularly alarming. To me it means that our Rebecca sees herself as a woman with a mission, a biblical mission, commanding a large following of fanatical delinquents. In other words, we are dealing with a religious activist. Her missions, as she sees them, are commanded by a supreme power to whom she owes allegiance.'

Sergeant Matthews looked duly impressed. The list of Rebecca's attributes was growing from day to day. First she had been an avenger, then an incendiary and now an extremist of the scriptural kind. Work in the Police force enlarged one's knowledge of human nature nearly every day.

'How do you see her, Matthews?'

'Who, me, Sir?'

'Yes, you, Matthews.'

'Oh, I don't know, Sir,' and then suddenly inspired, Sergeant Matthews said, 'Ugly Sir, very ugly with hair on her chin. Short and square with greying hair and middle-age spread.'

'Butch?' enquired Inspector Smithers.

'Something like that, Sir, I mean for a woman to be capable of such violence she's got to be something of a pervert.'

'There's drag, of course. Have you any thoughts about that?' asked Inspector Smithers.

'I can't say that I have, Sir,' replied Sergeant Matthews, 'but it's an interesting theory. It would have the merit of exonerating the fair sex. Women are gentle beings, aren't they?'

Inspector Smithers leant back in his chair. His features relaxed; a faint smile lent an unusual softness to his mouth

137

and eyes. *He* knew what she looked like, this Rebekah. Her breasts were small but firm, the buds of a warrior. She had long slender legs with well-shaped calves and fine ankles and she always wore a mini-skirt. She was tall, very tall, with bobbed hair, a gigantic Diana like the ones that deported themselves enigmatically across space-ships on interplanetary flights, fearfully competent, deliciously androgynous. Fleet of foot . . . she eluded him. Her stride was long and springy and at times, in his dejected moods, he could hear her laughing as she straddled the county . . . Then he was back on earth.

'What was the name of that policewoman, the one who helped to solve the Thornton case? You know . . . she had a hunch about one of the men who came forward to help with the enquiry. She thought he was too eager.'

'Compton, Sir?'

'Compton, that was it! Get her, will you? As a woman she may have a special insight into the misdeeds of another woman. And don't think I am being cynical, Matthews. I am no misogynist.'

'Beg your pardon, Sir?'

'Woman-hater in Greek. You've never studied Greek, have you, Matthews?'

'I can't say that I have, Sir.'

'I thought not.'

* * *

A few weeks later Inspector Smithers thought a recapitulation of all the data available on 'Rebecca' was required and he called his sergeant. 'Right, Matthews! That policewoman.'

'Compton, Sir?'

'Yes, Compton. Has she come up with anything?'

'Yes, Sir! I made a note of it. It's here somewhere in my book. Ah, here we are!'

Sergeant Matthews tore a piece of paper out of his notebook and handed it over to the Inspector.

'What the hell is this?', the Inspector asked fuming.

'French, Sir.'

'Of course, it's French. I can see it's French, but what the hell does it mean?'

'It means "look for the man", *cherchez l'homme* You've heard of *cherchez la femme*, "look for the woman"? Well, it's the same thing, only the sexes have been reversed. What WPC Compton thinks is that Rebecca may be doing all this to impress a man, who is not particularly interested in her; to attract his attention, if you like. All we've got to do is to trace this mystery man and he will lead us to Rebecca.'

Inspector Smithers threw his hands up in the air. It was all too much.

'In ancient Greece, Matthews, they had a monster called the Sphinx. It had the head of a young woman and it spoke in riddles and we in Great Britain have WPC Compton and it's a damned shame, Matthews, a damned shame!'

'Begging your pardon, Sir. May I be allowed to point out, to consult WPC Compton was your very own idea.'

'Yes, Matthews, I know it was my idea, but what I expected from her was a brilliant flash of feminine intuition, not a bloody riddle!'

PART II

16

Once again, Oliver was walking on familiar ground. The soil his footsteps sank into was sandy, fine in texture; he was able to tread lightly through it, admiring the scenery around him at the same time. If he chanced to look up, clumps of pine trees gracefully set against the horizon met his eyes. The pleasure he derived from looking at their dark tutelar shapes did not diminish with the passing of time.

He had almost reached the end of his trek. Another few yards through his favourite countryside, enjoying its blend of pastoral and marine charm, and he would be able to see Sergeant Wilkes with or without his recruits. He did not expect to stay long on the moor. Wilkes was still on active service; their exchanges had to be brief. Wilkes was a useful sort, he could supply valuable information. He got around a good deal in the course of his duties; he could run errands without attracting attention. Because he was still under the Colours, Oliver knew he could rely on him to be discreet.

Oliver had reached a desolate sand quarry where an old rusty tank lay scuppered like a steel dinosaur. Further away in the valley on the downside of Keeper's Moor, puffs of smoke rose here and there at intervals while Army vehicles tore about in a kind of chaotic quadrille.

'Ah, there you are, Sir! I'm sorry I'm late.'

143

'I see your chaps are playing with smoke grenades today, Sergeant. Pity I haven't got my binoculars with me'

'I don't think you'd be able to see the stick-on chest wounds from here, Sir, not even with binoculars. It's casualty simulation today; you know, three categories of blood and food colourings . . . .'

'I know, it's got to look real.'

'They had more or less the same sort of exercise on Salisbury Plain last week, with about 400 TA trainees. I was able to do a bit of business there for you, Sir, putting out feelers, you know . . . .'

'And was the result of your canvas satisfactory?'

'Capital, Sir. To tell you the truth, I was surprised. I never expected anything like that, I mean, apart from the volunteers who join to get away from the missus, a lot of the lads are keen to do something that toughens them up and gives them a chance to travel around a bit. Mind you, they had their Battalion Special the night before; that could account for their being in a cheerful mood.'

'Well, it can't be the food, can it, Sergeant? We all know what camp grub is like.'

'Oh, no, Sir, it can't be the food. What with the sausage rolls, the baked beans and the ginger nuts they brought back from the Crimea, the volunteers can do a lot better at their local, any time.'

'It can't be the money either . . . .'

'No, Sir! A lot of them were indignant when I suggested they were doing it for the tax-free bounty.'

'That leaves rape and plunder,' Oliver observed laughing.

'Oh, I don't think there's much chance of that on Salisbury Plain, Sir, not lumbering through mud in whacking big protective suits on chemical warfare training. Whatever it is, Sir, they keep coming back.'

'Yes, that is interesting,' Oliver commented thought-fully.' I suppose one could say that reservists actually want to become professional soldiers. Do you concur, Sergeant?'

'Heartily! Between you and me, Sir, they're the next best thing to mercenaries. The training is bloody good; they've got their kits and they're ready. A lot of them would like to go abroad for manoeuvres or even into combat. They envy their American counterparts who get called out every time there's a national disaster in the States.'

'All you've told me so far tallies with my own obser-vations. I can't thank you enough, Sergeant.'

'That's all right, Sir. Glad to be of service. It's time somebody sat up and took notice. I mean, with all these young trainees raring to go . . . .'

'You had better run along, Sergeant, or they'll be sending a search party to look for you.'

'Right-e-o, Sir!'

'I am looking into the problem of arms supplies . . . .'

'I'll keep my eyes and ears open. Goodbye, Sir, and God bless.'

'Goodbye, Sergeant.'

What Oliver felt he needed at this juncture was an assessment of reality, not God's blessing. Only an apprai-sal of reality would lead to a salubrious assertion of reality. To him, God was the freedom that had been granted to Satan to do evil. God was infinite, eternal and almighty for that reason. The likes of Sergeant Wilkes, who believed in a benevolent God, were necessary; they were the people through whom things happened because they were guided by simple convictions . . . . Alternately, because God was infinite, evil could expand ad infinitum. From time to time, men rebelled against the expansion which seemed to be governed by a longitudinal law of

145

gravity. They raised a banner; the Wilkes of this world rallied round and another crusade began. Then the ardour died down; the spread moved off again. Its progress was so insidious that it attracted the attention of only a few people. They in turn cried out, but they were voices crying in the wilderness, prophets without honour in their own country. Once again, the storm gathered. In desperation, people appealed to Heaven since in earth the rulers who were petitioned remained impervious. What appealing to heaven really meant was resorting to arms, invoking the God of War, not the Heavenly Father. When the language of Reason failed and people grew weary of endless idle talk, what alternative was there to the sword? When the iron hand of Injustice ruled, only tempered steel could break its tyranny.

The stream of democracy had run on from the pure waters of its spring to the polluted levels of its spate, rushing headlong heedless of contamination. Lip-service was still being paid to democracy as to some grotesque idol that had grown fat beyond recognition on its own fleshpots. Words replaced deeds. The problems of millions of people were treated like refuse by methods of waste disposal. Daily they were hauled in front of the public by the media; exposed, thrashed out and decomposed, they ended up buried under an avalanche of verbal sewerage where it was assumed they would safely lie, far from the uncontaminated air of problem-free areas. Social injustice brought outbreaks of lawlessness in its wake and more verbosity to deal with them. People started claiming rights they had not got and ignoring the ones they had. Their self-deception on that score was total and it could be said that as a political system democracy was being carried to absurd lengths in an anarchical cloud-cuckoo-land . . . .

Here on Keeper's Down, surrounded by so much

natural beauty, Oliver could give vent to his bitterest thoughts. Above all, he could grieve. He could weep over his country's fate, mourn the demise of its sanity. He marvelled that he could still love England with the same fervour, now he could see her flaws and disabilities, as he did when he served in Germany and distance idealized her image. His idealism might have been crushed since he had returned home, but not his fervour. He still yearned for England, or rather for her restored effigy, as he could picture it in his mind's eye; on the ascendant, she became his lodestar, beckoning him on. Only occasionally, when he was very tired, or the way ahead seemed fraught with too much strife, did its scintillant appeal shine through less brightly. He was a tender-hearted man and he baulked at the thought of the cruel divisions which any drastic initiative would inevitably create between men. He knew he would have to take unpopular measures. When, as a benign visionary, he had serene moments, he felt confident that commonsense would prevail and courage fly to its aid to implement change. At the other end of the scale, when anger got the better of him, he knew he would, for justice's sake, be capable of hardening his heart and smite without demur.

Walking and thinking, he had absent-mindedly reached the spot where he had first met Stella; he recognized it quite by chance, so engrossed was he in tumultuous cogitation. He remembered her fall had taken place in a clearing with a slender tree like a silver birch to which he had tied her horse; he also recollected having propped her up against a moss-grown stone. These were the two things that jogged his memory – the tree and the stone. On that very same day he had seen Sergeant Wilkes for the first time and been struck by his perspicacity. Wilkes was a man of a completely different stamp from Nash or even Bates. He was married but had no offspring.

147

His recruits were his children; the authority he exerted over them was that of a *pater*, strict but fair. Over the years he had acquired an almost uncanny insight into the mentality of young soldiers. He elicited obedience not through fear but through paternal foresight; this understanding gave the lads confidence and made them compliant.

Wilkes had given Stella a piece of fatherly advice. 'You should wear a crash helmet, Miss.' Down-to-earth and concerned, that was Wilkes.

Oliver sighed. Would that he could describe Stella in terms as explicit and simple as the ones he had just applied to that personable sergeant! Metaphysical considerations, abstract concepts, all had to go by the board when depicting Stella. The question of prime importance was not 'what was Stella like?' but rather 'what to do with Stella?' She seemed to be completely divorced from the practicalities of daily life, even from personal relationships; to function in a world of her own, with its private interests, its intimate joys (her sorrows were by contrast easier to understand). At times, he felt tempted to bully her to make her snap out of her seclusion, for her own good, or was it for her own good? She never appeared unhappy; that was the most puzzling thing about her, she never complained. She just existed in conformity with herself midway between known situations . . . .

Having her in the house did not help. He found her extremely attractive, soft and quiet. The softness of her body and the quietness of her temperament were not the least features of the attraction as far as he was concerned. She was not child-like, possibly she was too well-read to be puerile. Intellectually speaking, he found her, in fact, very mature. If she got excited about anyone, it was always some character in a book or in a painting. She would embark on a perceptive explanation of their behaviour.

148

She would get carried away, smiling and laughing, as she delved deeper and deeper into their idiosyncrasies. What moved him beyond words was that her character studies always started from sound premises; she was instinctively on the side of life; she took the fullness of life as her criterion.

He was charmed by her. More and more often, when he returned from his military explorations, some of them quite hazardous, he caught himself looking forward to finding her in the house. Once he came back from a training session in Northumberland and she wasn't in. He suffered such an inordinate sense of disappointment that he blamed himself for not getting things in perspective. Either the training of guerrillas in Northumbria was too strenuous (he was getting too old for Spartan discipline) or his desire for female company had been repressed for too long; it now rebelled against self-control and found a conveniently close repository in Stella . . . .

Little did he know when he and Wilkes got Stella up from the ground in this very spot, after she had fallen from her horse, that the sorry sight she looked then would one day be superseded by a presence from which mystery and charm emanated in equal degree. He turned over all these thoughts in his mind, but was none the wiser for the threshing. Perhaps the best course for the moment was to adopt a fatalistic attitude, to tolerate a day-to-day acceptance of the situation, let things drift as they were, for what they were worth. Anyway, Stella might not be staying at the Masseys' much longer. She had been offered a post in London and kept saying that she would take it up as soon as she felt stronger. He did not like to ask, but he hoped she would not move to London: he couldn't bear the thought of her living in digs in the capital. Although her accommodation at the Masseys' was not entirely satisfactory, at least it attached her to a household. There

149

was a warm, lived-in atmosphere around her and the Masseys were the most unobtrusive hosts one could wish for: thoughtful, generous and discreet, they let Stella be. After her near-fatal accident at Cowes, they never mentioned the name of their niece Pandora, although they had been instrumental in introducing her to Stella.

17

During the night Stella woke up to the sound of her own sobs. Unable to bear the grief she had experienced in her sleep, she flung back the bedclothes and rushed out of her room barefooted. She slept in a kind of disused basement den in Oliver Carrington's friends' house; the place had once served as a playroom for their children before they left home. Still crying she groped up the basement stairs in the dark. She thought Oliver slept in a bedroom on the first floor, but she wasn't sure. When she crossed the hall, she realized that she had left her wrap behind. It was too late now to go back for it. Oliver had heard a noise; he was leaning over the bannister to see what the trouble was. Stella ran upstairs to meet him.

'Please listen to me,' she pleaded, 'listen to me!'

'Stella, what's the matter? You've been crying! Calm down, you'll wake everybody up.'

'I dreamt I was back at Darley Hall.'

Oliver took her by the hand and led her gently to his room. He closed the door in case she became hysterical and roused the household. He noticed she was shivering. He pulled a blanket off the bed and wrapped it round her thin, heaving body.

'Sit in this chair and tell me all about it. But first dry your tears, I can't bear tears.'

She picked up the hem of her nightdress and wiped her face with it.

151

'I dreamt I was back at Darley Hall. An angry spirit walked abroad with unspeakable rage. I stood on the bottom step of the big oak staircase in the main hall. Before going upstairs, I looked down at the door of the basement kitchen which was concealed in shadows, then I looked across the hall at the front door. Both doors were shut but somehow the knowledge brought me no comfort. An uncanny silence pervaded the atmosphere. Sliding my hand on the rail, I began my ascent, taking great care not to make a noise, constantly looking up and down as I progressed up the stairs. Rays of light shone through the stained glass window above the first landing; the beams, neither strong nor weak, gave no clue as to the time of day. A feeling of timelessness hung on the air. Of course, I knew where I was; I knew the place. I had climbed that same staircase time and time again, carrying books in the course of my duties, up and down from the library to the headmistress's study and from there to the classrooms that fanned out around it on the first landing. But this time things were different. I was all awareness, all conscious-ness, bent on obeying a call which came from above.

'I cringed as I walked past Miss Beaumont's study; the door was ajar as it had been that day when I surprised her and Mrs Cunningham locked in loving embrace. I rushed along the landing, almost missing the bottom step of the next flight of stairs, in my haste to get away from that vision, on to the brighter heights which beckoned me from above. I paused breathless on the second landing. The doors of the dormitories were all shut. Their flat, inert surfaces stared at me like so many enigmas I could not solve. Forcing myself to lift my right foot on the first step of the last flight of stairs I had to climb, I laid my hand on the bannister and gripping it looked upwards. A voice within me had just said, "Don't look down now!" A maelstrom of hostile influences had built up in the lower

152

regions of the house, threatening to engulf me. Resisting their pull, I started going up to the top floor. When I reached it, without any hesitation I went over to a door at the far end of the corridor and turned the china knob. At first I could not see anything; then slowly objects began to detach themselves from the gloom – brass bedsteads, broken wash basins; some of those had been ripped off the walls and hung with disconnected copper pipes drooping at their sides. Here and there the darkness was lit by white sheets which had been thrown over beds; the stuffing of their mattresses had been chewed by rats; bits of it scurried about across the floor boards with balletic liveliness in the draught brought in by me from the corridor.

'Quickly I shut the door. I started making my way to one of the mansard windows. I knew exactly where I was going. Fortunately for me, the window seat of that particular window had not collapsed, I was able to climb on it. A wave of happiness surged through my whole being as I looked down into the grounds. The view had not changed at all! Its proportions, the arrangement of all its composite parts, still spelt out perfection. It was as though Nature and the hand of man had collaborated to create an enchanting sight, for all times. As it had shown itself to my young admiring eyes all those years ago, so it presented itself to my gaze in the dream and the feelings it conveyed of beauty, order, tranquillity were the same as they had been then. They overwhelmed me with love. It was easy to see why in my salad days I had been deceived into thinking the view and all the emotions it inspired reflected the natural order of things, the whole of life . . . . I must have started sobbing then.'

Oliver could see the narration of the dream had exhausted her. He took both her hands in his and pulled her up from the chair.

'Come, I'll take you back to your room. You'll be able

153

to rest now you've unburdened yourself.'

'Do you think she killed her?'

'Who?'

'Miss Beaumont.'

'You mean Mrs Cunningham kill Miss Beaumont?'

'Yes.'

'Of course not! The coroner concluded death from natural causes. Miss Beaumont died of cardiac arrest.'

'Sometimes, I think my mind has been poisoned . . . .'

'You know,' Oliver replied cheerfully, inflecting his voice with as much confidence as he could, 'the mind has its own wonderful ways of cleansing itself. It has safety valves. Dreams and nightmares are two of them.'

She let herself be led down the passage. Oliver said nothing more. Wistfully he pursued his own train of thought as he escorted her back to her room in the basement . . . , Darley Hall had been gutted by flames . . .

The fire that destroyed it had raged with an intensity commensurate with the horror the house inspired in his mind and in the mind of the people who set it ablaze. Their common purpose had been to obliterate it as the seat of nefarious influences, but it was clear that fire could never purify the house in Stella's memory, never erase its shame – what had been, had been.

18

Oliver returned to Aldershot in a sombre mood. The weather in Northumbria had broken. Gale force winds with thunderstorms and hail stones had stretched the men's patience to breaking-point. Oliver had slept under canvas with them, sharing all the hardships the bad weather had brought to their punishing schedule in the field. At first a spell of windless dry weather had brought ideal conditions and Oliver had taken advantage of it to intensify after-dark patrol training. He loved those serene winter nights, between the full moon, and the last quarter, when the sky was clear and the stars' geometrical patterns drew man's gaze heavenward, when moonlight cast its long still shadows on the ground, adding to the quietness of the nocturnal scene and to its treachery for the men on the prowl, making them fearful of ambush .... But endurance tests could not be put off indefinitely. Adverse weather conditions helped to harden the men who had been condemned to enforced idleness through redundancy; when the weather broke, Oliver had to announce the start of endurance tests. As the weather deteriorated, so tempers grew thin. What had started as a murmur, in a short while became a loud wave of discontent. Oliver saw clearly where his course lay – he would have to resort to stern plain speaking before more men were sent up north to undergo training. Unpleasant as the task was, it did not plunge him into as much gloom as the prospect of discussing 'Operation Gamekeeper' with the men. He wished that he could have collected a platoon or two and dealt with the problem himself in semi-secrecy, but the spirit of the movement, its very ethos, precluded it; if the men found out that they had been kept out of it, their confidence in him would be undermined. Sergeant Bates had been instructed to call a gathering of the troops for a brief on the operation. Rebecca Flemington had been invited to attend too. Oliver felt he owed it to her to involve her more in underground activities. Of late she had matured a lot; she seemed far less flippant.

When he caught sight of her in the assembly, he was not at all displeased to see her. Somehow, he felt she would approve of the hard line he was about to take. Unenthusiastically he began his address. 'The purpose of this meeting is to give me a chance to discuss "Operation Gamekeeper" with you all. The operation has been set up because we must put a stop to the illicit practices some of us have discovered during the course of our training in Northumbria. Local reprobates have been taking advantage of the trust the conservation authorities placed in them to teach the young their evil skills, unchallenged in out-of-the-way places. We must deal with them for security reasons. The booby-traps used in military conflicts are part of the arsenal of war and as such can be considered legitimate hazards. Snares and traps are illegal; camouflaged in the countryside they could inflict serious injuries to men training in the field, apart from submitting animals to a cruel death. To carry out a mopping up operation of this nature, we need a special task force. Volunteers must know the area well and be able to reconnoitre and act singly if necessary. Any suggestions?'

'What about Nash, Sir?' Sergeant Bates asked. 'He's not here tonight but I can speak for him. He knows the coast well and he still speaks with a Geordie accent.'

'I know Nash was born in Newcastle, but he was sixteen when he joined up. How much does he actually remember? We are dealing with a particular stretch of coastline, between Seahouses and Beadnell.'

'I know, Sir, but Nash's parents still live in Newcastle; his brother never left the area, they could prove useful.'

Oliver hesitated. When Nash was made redundant he was still a corporal, after twelve years in the Army . . . .

'I'm not very keen. No, let him act as a scout and get Smiley.'

'Smiley!' Sergeant Bates could not help exclaiming.

'Yes, Smiley! Apparently, when he worked for the Contras in Nicaragua, it was common knowledge that he killed smiling, when he got really incensed.'

'Sadism?' asked Rebecca.

'No, satisfaction at a job well done. Let him bring his accordion; he'll cheer the men up in the evening; the weather can be pretty dismal up there.'

'It's funny, to me he looks more like a cistercian monk than an executioner,' remarked Rebecca. 'What about his dog? Surely, you're not going to let him take that with him as well? It might disappear down a peat bog and never come up again!'

'Miss Flemington has an excellent memory,' said Oliver turning towards the men, 'we ought to make use of it . . . . I now want to deal with the complaints that keep reaching my ears about the training sessions in Northumberland. I hear rumours about the track along Hadrian's Wall being too muddy for eight-mile runs in full pack; about the scarp face of fells being too steep for climbing or the sand dunes that back the shore too slippery for crawling – they have damp hollows and not enough marram grass to cling to . . . . All these "gripes" are ludicrous and not worthy of an enquiry. Training will

157

continue on the lines indicated in the manual you have been issued with. Discipline must be unyielding if the acquisition of field skills is to be stepped up. Bad apples will be booted out regardless of rank, record, length of service, redundancy and family cares. Pass the word on, Sergeant.'

'Yes, Sir.'

'Now for the good news. We have been fortunate in intercepting a consignment of Ruger 337 magnums and Hecker and Koch machine-guns destined for Northern Ireland. I trust that most of you are familiar with these weapons. Those who aren't must see Sergeant Bates about it forthwith. Time is running out. I rely on you all to honour your pledge of solidarity from now on, come what may.'

A devout quietness fell on the assembly, then gradually the word 'solidarity' issued from the lips of a few soldiers and broke the silence. As with the intoning of a chant, so the volume of sound increased as other men joined in to add their pledge until the whole place blared with the repetitive echo of that one word 'solidarity' to hearten the most timid amongst them.

In spite of herself, Rebecca felt deeply moved. A watershed had just been crossed; old selves had been sloughed off: everybody, herself included, had bade farewell to a past that looked shabby in retrospect. For the first time she felt there was a glorious future in the making, calling them all forward. She could almost feel its pull. All blurred outlines had hardened. Schemes which yesterday seemed outrageous now fitted into the realm of possibilities with merciless logic. The wheels of time's tumbrel creaked towards an irresistible goal.

Not that she felt unhappy about any of the punitive acts she had perpetrated in the recent past – the wreck of the *Amaryllis,* the raid on the bank at Windsor, arson at

Darley Hall – she could not disown any of them. She had performed all three wilfully as rites of passage to gain entrance into an arcanum. But now that she had put them safely behind her, they seemed eccentric, even meanly mercenary, the manifestations of that old wayward self she had just shed. She had been converted into a new person, not dramatically by a flash of lightning on the road to Damascus, but modestly by what she could only describe as grace for want of a better word. Through grace she had been granted Unification with Congress; the futility of her former life had been borne away. The new Rebecca was ready to take her place in the rank and file and therein to find liberation, not in any fashionable way . . . .

Oliver had sent the men away. He was now standing with a small group of people Rebecca had never seen before. Some wore battledress, others were in muftie. An animated conversation was taking place between them. Oliver chanced to look up and saw her watching. He excused himself and walked over to where she stood.

'You must come and meet those men: they were fellow officers of mine in the tanks in Germany. They're the best there are.'

She smiled and crossed the floor with Oliver.

'Gentlemen, I'd like to introduce Rebecca Flemington. Her father was General Flemington, late of the Army of the Rhine. Rebecca, this is Guy Tomlinson, Larry Davies, Simon Roberts, Peter Holmes, Desmond "Binky" Lakin . . . .'

Rebecca shook hands with a string of names. She had a good memory for names, but there were too many of them to memorize in one sweep. They all looked young; here and there a stockier figure indicated more mature years. She did not think that she had very much to say to them. When her father was alive, when she was a young girl just

159

out of school, the company of such men was a frequent occurrence which titillated her; it helped her discover her femininity. Her father, to protect her against her own silliness, always began his introductions by saying that she had grown up without a mother, thereby warding off all the young bloods in his regiment. She used to resent it bitterly; she felt it cast an aspersion on her . . . . She was waiting for Oliver to say something equally damning.

'Rebecca has been mixed up in this business from its incipience. She has contributed to the success of several initiatives, which encourages me to believe that she will be a great asset to the movement when we start the ball rolling.'

A burst of energetic clapping met Oliver's words. Rebecca returned the compliment by clapping too. Oliver paused, looked round at the men who were facing him and went on.

'How to dissociate practicality from morality in a cause like ours is devilishly difficult.'

'Hear, Hear!' they all muttered.

'That we must endeavour to do so is imperative – we must not give our opponents a handle to browbeat us by making out we're some sort of fanatical society. So for the practical considerations first: as I see it, we, the regular Army, are nearly all jobless and we have no future. The Territorials, the volunteer forces, because they are cost-effective, will play an expanding role in future defence requirements. Not all of us ex-officers are homeless, but all the troops are; the few who aren't are forced to live in an environment they loathe. That makes for an awful lot of discontent. As a regular land force, we can duplicate most civilian jobs and public services – Police, Ambulance, mechanics, electricians, computer experts, transport, catering, mail, name it, we've got it or we can supplement. We could provide all our chaps with jobs at different echelons.

'Now for the moral considerations. The King's last piece of indiscretion concerning his private life has thrown Royal ethics into discredit. The King has made a mockery of his marriage vows and put the Church of England in a quandary – don't forget the Church and the Crown are under mutual obligation. The King can no longer honourably claim to be the Defender of the Faith. Apart from being the temporal head of the Church, the King is also Head of the Armed Forces. If he has become unfit for the first office, the question is, is he fit for the second one, or are the two part and parcel of Kingship and would the one invalidate the other? And secondly, can we as soldiers, continue to honour our oath of allegiance to a flawed monarch? Gentlemen, Miss Flemington, you must draw your own conclusions.'

Guy Tomlinson stepped forward a few paces. He was not very tall. His feet, Rebecca thought, were rather large for his height, but they gave him a stable appearance.

'I think I speak for all of us,' he began, 'when I say that the brief Oliver Carrington has just given us sums up the situation very accurately.'

'Hear, hear!' they shouted unanimously.

'The general feeling in the Army seems to be that the situation is likely to get worse, though how no-one can really tell. Once the rot has set in, the process of disintegration is irreversible. It could have something to do with the social trends of the times, some upheaval in the human psyche, casting off outdated slants in order to move towards new ones, a migratory impulse perhaps, a legacy from the previous nomadic experience in the great forward march of mankind . . . .'

'The aberrations of one era giving way to the aberrations of the next,' commented Simon Roberts.

'That was a very cynical aside, Simon,' observed Guy

161

Tomlinson.

'Are people happier for it? I mean, exchanging values that appease one's conscience for standards that don't necessarily do so?' asked Desmond Lakin.

'I think we're digressing into the sphere of social history,' interrupted Oliver, 'we ought not to lose sight of some basic facts of human life, biological ones, if you like, that men must work in order to feed themselves and their young. We ought not to philosophize too much.'

'I agree,' said Larry Davies, 'we have a huge practical problem to solve, how to provide work for ourselves and our troops. But do correct me if I'm wrong, Oliver, but I thought your initial motive was moral indignation at the plight of the Army . . . . I mean, you had to have an ideological spring of action to stir the men up in the first place.'

Oliver frowned.

'You make it sound so mercenary, Larry, like some cheap propaganda stunt.'

'Far from me the notion that you were the type of rabble-rousing lunatic described by the Press, but what's your rallying cry going to be? I mean, if I understand the drift of your address to us, your scenario for the solution to our problem is pretty hectic?'

'Yes, it is,' replied Oliver.

'In that case, I think we ought to confer carefully, don't you?' asked Simon Roberts. 'Is Miss Flemington staying?'

'She can, if she wants to . . . . Rebecca?'

'Yes, I'm staying.'

'That makes you a conspirator,' laughed Peter Holmes, 'and a very dangerous one; good looks in a woman make her twice as treacherous!'

Rebecca gave a melancholy smile. She had passed the stage when that kind of flattery coming from a younger man tickled her vanity.

162

'Let's be blunt,' said Guy Tomlinson. 'What you would like, Oliver, is to see us all back in business.'

'Yes, that's right,' Oliver answered.

'The King, you pointed out, is head of the armed forces . . . .'

'Yes . . . .'

'He is also the temporal head of the Church and you no longer consider him worthy of either title?'

'Yes, that is correct,' replied Oliver.

'Are you suggesting,' Guy Tomlinson went on, 'that we ought to get rid of the King?'

'Yes, I am.'

A long silence ensued and Rebecca wondered who would be the first one to break it.

'And Parliament?' whispered Larry Davies, 'It meets on the personal summons of the Sovereign . . . .'

'Its normal life is five years. This Parliament is only two years old. Besides, does Parliament provide a more representative cross-section of the people of England than the Army?'

Rebecca saw the look of astonishment on all their faces and she felt sorry for them. She was probably the only person there who could not be shocked by this original slant on the Army. She had had a head start on all these men. She had had time to get used to Oliver's incredible powers of perception, to his scalpel-sharp faculty for extracting essential facts from the formality that concealed them. She had got used to hearing the truth.

Larry Davies was the first one to react.

'You said "the people of England", not the British people?'

'The Scots are on the warpath; they want their own parliament. The union is in jeopardy. We ought to think of an independent England.'

'The rose between two thorns . . . ,' muttered Peter

163

Holmes.

'You mean, just England and St George? Scrap Patrick and Andrew?' enquired Desmond Lakin.

'Something like that,' replied Oliver.

'It's not exactly a novel idea, is it?' asked Simon Roberts.

'No,' answered Oliver, 'but it is timely.'

'To go back to the King,' said Guy Tomlinson, 'if we raise a hue and cry about his disqualifications and the clamour becomes alarmingly loud . . . .'

'The Government will probably organize a referendum,' replied Oliver, 'or the media launch one of their opinion polls in true democratic fashion. Here one of the dangers will be maudlin sentimentality. People will start feeling sorry for the King; they'll conjure up Fair Play, the hallmark of English gentlemen. He's not such a bad chap after all. Why not keep him, poor bloke? He's making the best of a bad job. Why shouldn't he have a bit of fun on the side, like the rest of us?'

'How can one avoid that?' asked Peter Holmes. 'The average Englishman is mawkish.'

Oliver's face took on a wistful expression.

'If we challenge the King about his reputation when his popularity is at a low ebb, he will stand down in favour of his eldest son and we shall have missed an opportunity. If we insist the King is answerable personally and must be arraigned . . . .'

'People will say we're settling up old scores,' remarked Guy Tomlinson.

'Seeking justice is more like it, but please let me finish, Guy. If we insist, as I was saying, loyalists will rally round the young prince to make the Crown secure for him. There'll be a tightening-up of royalist prejudice and that could mean civil war. Is that what we want? Turmoil is one thing, bloodshed another.'

'The last thing we want,' said Peter Holmes, 'is a revival of royalist fervour, the consequences would be disastrous for the nation.'

'What do you suggest, Oliver?' asked Guy Tomlinson.

'A coup to depose the King and abolish monarchy,' replied Oliver. 'Abolish the Crown,' Oliver pressed on to make the most of the element of surprise, 'and you abolish government. Abolish the Crown and you give back the Church its spiritual independence. Abolish the Crown and you give back the Army its dignity. Abolish the Crown and you turn passive subjects into active citizens. Abolish the Crown and you wipe out a legacy of feudal practices. Abolish the Crown and you enable England to step boldly into the 21st century rather than remissly.'

Those words assaulted the ears of Oliver's audience and the impact of their delivery stunned them into shocked silence. Simon Roberts was the first one to recover speech.

'And how do you propose to do that?' he asked Oliver. 'Issue the King with an ultimatum?'

'You've obviously not been listening to what I've been saying. Turning to the King would be a complete waste of time. He has a high opinion of himself and of his estate. He will try and hang on to royal privileges, if not for himself at least for his son, especially if he feels he can call upon a loyalist militia to protect his House. No, we must take Buckingham Palace by storm and hold the King under house arrest until such time that he and his family can be relegated for good.'

'What about the Prime Minister?' asked Larry Davies. 'He will want to make a statement in Parliament. Will you arrest him as well?'

'Why this obsession with Parliament, Larry? It's become an arena for political mud-slinging. The people of England must sit in Parliament, not the politicians – the soldiers and the workers together in Common council. No,

I tell you, the King is the key to everything. Depose the King and there's an end to government. It is His Majesty's government. All the ministers, including the Home Secretary and the Lord Chancellor, are Crown ministers; I needn't remind you about that. Abolish the Crown and you abolish government and Parliamentary legislation as well – the supreme legislative authority in the United Kingdom is the King in Parliament. The only thing that will stand, mercifully, is common law, but it won't be administered from Crown Courts.'

'Have you thought who or what will govern in the place of His Majesty's Government? Who will maintain law and order, once the Home Secretary and the Lord Chancellor have gone?' asked Guy Tomlinson.

'Guy,' replied Oliver, 'at the beginning of this meeting you said something about my wanting to see us all back in business. So why the question now? Government, not just soldiering, will be our business, by the solemn engagement of the Army.'

Guy Tomlinson shook his head while staring at the floor.

'I see . . . are you sure there are enough of us to cope?'

'Good God, yes!' exclaimed Oliver. 'You know as well as I do that thousands of men have been repatriated from garrisons overseas. There are too many regiments to redeploy, too few barracks to house the troops, not enough jobs in civvy street for men to be willing to resign, so inevitably there will be more cuts and more chances for us to raise new supplies of men.'

Guy Tomlinson cleared his throat.

'Talking of recruiting, rumours are going round about the type of fighting personnel you enlist. People are talking about riff-raff.'

'I don't go for a particular type of person. The men I tend to select have the defects of their qualities; the

166

majority of them are ex-servicemen, anyway. Remember Hobart? He was a typical example of a soldier who was put aside on the strength of the defects of his qualities. What part would the tanks have played in the last war if Churchill had not requested that Hobart should be recalled? "Remember Hobart" my father used to tell me. For years I was haunted by Hobart and his fate. When Churchill had him recalled, he was a corporal in the Home Guard. General Hobart, a corporal in the Home Guard! The man was a visionary, possibly the only genius the Royal Tank Corps ever had!'

'All right, all right,' Guy Tomlinson urged, 'it's very upsetting, but then history teems with visionaries like Hobart who were ostracized because their vision upset less gifted people, and some of them never got recalled. At least Hobart had his chance. If you are happy with the type of men you recruit and you can guarantee their loyalty, that's fine by me. Binky, Larry, Simon, Peter, what do you say?'

'I don't see why not,' replied Larry Davies. 'Sometimes headstrong men make very good soldiers once their energies have been channelled, no matter what background they come from.'

'We're all in agreement,' announced Desmond Lakin.

'Good,' said Oliver, 'I don't want to hear another word about it. Another source of manpower we can tap is the Territorial Army.'

'Good Lord, Oliver!' exclaimed Simon Roberts. 'How many more blows on the head will you deal us tonight? We're all going to need stiff cordials before long'

'I'm sorry you think I'm clouting you too hard, but this isn't the time for drawing-room niceties.'

'How do you know the Territorials will be willing to join in this venture?' asked Peter Holmes.

'I know they will.'

167

'What makes you so sure?'

'Well, for one thing, we trained them. Furthermore, a lot of them were disappointed that they weren't sent to the Gulf at the time of the war with Iraq.'

'Surely, the kind of operation you have in mind does not compare with Desert Storm! It's a different keg of powder,' observed Desmond Lakin.

Oliver smiled.

'You'll find that once you've trained a civilian to use a gun and can wind him up with the proper pyrotechnics, his fingers will be itching to pull the trigger, whatever the call, especially if he's been standing in front of a machine in a factory all bloody week.'

'You're probably right,' Simon Roberts said, 'It's just that in the past one was led to believe our chaps were not killers, anyway that's what our elders used to say.'

'Times have changed,' Oliver went on. 'There's the tedium of life in Britain on the one hand and violence on television on the other. Provide an adventure playground and the upshot may surprise you. So you see, and I hope I have convinced you, the fighting force is not a problem; it is considerable in strength and in great shape. The men I drill in Northumberland are standing up well to the rigorous exercises of their training. No; the major problem that confronts us is one of logistics, how to move tanks up to the capital for C-Day . . . .'

19

'Sergeant Bates requesting permission to report on "Operation Gamekeeper", Sir.'

'Permission eagerly granted, Sergeant,' replied Oliver smiling, 'I am as impatient to hear your news as you are to impart it.'

'Thank you, Sir. I arrived back in Aldershot last night, after having spent a week at camp in Northumberland, as you requested, Sir. The purpose of my visit was to investigate the progress of "Operation Gamekeeper." As you know. Sir, our chaps had found snares and traps dotted about the countryside as they carried out their training exercises. There were lots of complaints about this ugly-looking ironmongery; the number of absentees grew from day to day, and by the time I arrived, it had reached an alarming rate. In addition, every day, twice a day, always at the same time, mornings and late afternoons, shots rang out . . . .'

'What kind of shots, Sergeant?'

'Firearms shots, not air-guns, real gunshots and they weren't fired by our chaps. One day, shortly after my arrival at camp, at the time when normally we heard shots, no shot rang out but we heard instead some very distinctive thuds which we were able to identify immediately – they, whoever they were, poachers or gamekeepers, had fitted their guns with silencers. Whether they got wise

169

to the fact that the regular occurrence of the shooting had attracted our attention, we shall never know. Putting two and two together, we came to the conclusion that they were determined to carry on with whatever they were doing and that they didn't want us to know about it, or they would not have mounted silencers on the guns. We knew that they were about somewhere. We also knew that they had sniffed us out and the situation became down-right uncomfortable. The men on night patrol became edgy.

'Then Smiley arrived. He had brought his accordion all right, but he also had his dog with him and that I hadn't bargained for; I mean, dogs do bark, don't they, and in view of the situation, I didn't think that was on. But Smiley being Smiley, you know what I mean, Sir, the kind that gets away with murder, there was no question of sending the dog away to boarding kennels – Smiley wouldn't hear of it; not only that but he kept threatening anyone who tried to get near the dog, and we all knew what Smiley was capable of. Well, a dog's nature being what it is, after having been kept on the leash for weeks on end to draw the crowds to Smiley's accordion playing, the dog took to wandering off more and more frequently and for longer and longer escapades, until one day it did not return. I was very angry about it. We armed ourselves to the teeth – I don't know what made us do it, but you know how future events sometimes cast a shadow in front of them, to precede them so to speak. We were all on edge. Recent happenings had unnerved us, I suppose; the repetition of the shots, twice a day, quite close, but how close we did not know; the reports varied each time in sharpness and we had never seen anyone carrying a gun on our regular outings in daylight. I think we all knew that it wasn't just the dog we were going after. Well, we'd left Beadnell Bay behind us and were walking northwards

170

when we came to a desolate stretch of sand. Suddenly, in a hollow in the dunes, I saw poor little Slim's head sticking out of a clump of reeds; it had a bullet hole through it. Smiley bent down to pick it up and to our horror as he lifted the dog off the ground he brought up with it a snare like shark's teeth that was attached to the dog's legs . . . .'

'What, both of them?'

'Yes, Sir, both of them; they were just a mangled mess. The dog must have struggled to free itself . . . . Smiley turned pale. We could see he was enraged and it wasn't a pretty sight, what with him always looking so cheerful. He insisted on bringing the dog back to camp and there we buried him, minus his legs.'

'What do you mean, "minus his legs"?'

'Well, Sir, we had to blast the snare open and as it blew up, so the dog's legs flew off and we couldn't find a single trace of them anywhere.'

'Did you see any footprints in the sand? Somebody must have gone up to the dog to shoot it through the head.'

'No, Sir, nothing, except some funny stripes about a yard away, as though somebody had swept the dune with twigs.'

'To erase tracks?'

'That's what it looked like, Sir.'

'Could one of our men have found the dog in the trap and shot it?'

'I don't think so, Sir. Nobody came forward. We wondered if the shots we heard on a regular basis every day had anything to do with it.'

'You mean the countryside would be littered with the bodies of dogs that had been shot through the head after having been caught in traps? It doesn't make sense! Why ensnare them in the first place?'

'I don't know, Sir. the world is full of lunatics. Perhaps

171

whoever did it had a guilty conscience and went back afterwards to put the animal out of its misery or a relative did it, behind the guilty party's back to keep their nasty habit quiet.'

'Firing shots twice a day, always at the same time, isn't exactly a good way of keeping things quiet, is it, Sergeant?'

'No, Sir, it isn't.'

'Did Smiley know about the snares and traps?'

'Of course, Sir. As soon as he arrived I informed him about them myself. I put him in the picture right from the beginning. I explained how the snares and traps had been discovered by our chaps during the course of training in the sand dunes. I also told him about the strange gathering our men had stumbled upon one day at nightfall when they were practising target spotting on one of the low headlands.'

'You told him what they saw?'

'Exactly as they saw it, Sir; the older men showing the youths in the group how to set snares and traps, unaware our men were spying on them. Smiley asked me if we knew who these rogues were. I told him they were professional gamekeepers, quite well-known locally, and that two of them had since been identified as Reserve Wardens employed by the National Trust. He smiled; somehow the idea seemed to tickle his fancy. I told him you wanted him to make the countryside safe for our men.

'Well, after that, we didn't see much of him. He'd come back to camp every night with the dog at heel and entertain us on the accordion. Nash, who was scouting for him, didn't say much. Every time I'd ask him how Smiley was getting on he'd reply "like a kipper in Craster, Serg." Bloody Geordie! I expect what he meant was that Smiley had no problem sneaking around; kippers in Craster are thirteen a dozen, cured over oak chips; you should ask

Miss Flemington to bring you some back next time she comes down south on leave, Sir.'

'Yes, Sergeant. Proceed.'

'After the dog was killed, Smiley said he didn't need Nash as a guide any more; he knew his way around and would work solo. He seemed a changed man.'

'What do you mean? Smiley was always . . . Smiley.'

'He didn't play the accordion any more for one thing, and he didn't smile at all. Miss Flemington was reported to have said that Smiley gave her the creeps, and she took to keeping a rifle by her side at night. Well, two days before a company of fully trained recruits were due to swap places with a new batch of trainees from the South, Smiley disappeared.'

'Disappeared?'

'He didn't report for duties in the morning and didn't answer the roll-call in the evening.'

'Did you send out a search party for him?'

'Oh, yes, Sir.'

'Well?'

'They didn't find him, but they found something else instead. The young soldier who ran back to base to fetch me was in such a state, I had to discharge him there and then so that he could get cleaned up. I'm a soldier, Sir, and I've seen casualties, but this was something else.'

'Smiley had done his job?'

'Oh, yes, Sir, you could say that.'

'Smiling?'

'I'd say. In a dip between two sand dunes, covered with reeds and surrounded by an assortment of gins of all shapes and sizes, two elderly men lay side by side. Their hands had been tied together at the wrists; they were manacled by a springe like the one in which the poor dog had died. Both men had been . . . .'

'Shot through the head?'

173

'No, Sir, garrotted.'

Oliver's face did not register the look of surprise Sergeant Bates expected. If one thought about it, considering the Spanish influence in South America, it was not surprising after all that Smiley favoured that form of penalty.

'Did you make an announcement?'

'There was no need, Sir. The news went through the camp like wild fire. Needless to say, we shifted sites immediately, moving back to C Base away from the coast. I took it upon myself to discharge the fully trained recruits, including Nash, there and then, rather than have them move twice.'

'You did rightly, Sergeant. I dare say they'll take it upon themselves to inform their comrades down here about the successful outcome of "Operation Gamekeeper"?'

'Yes, Sir. I don't think there is any need for you to issue a statement, not just yet anyway. Everybody's been a bit rattled. I should let the dust settle, if I were you.'

20

The minute Stella woke up the knowledge that she had had a very strange dream during the night nudged her consciousness. Even the ray of light shining through the curtains, from the lamppost on the pavement outside her room, did not distract her from acknowledging the presence of the dream at the fore of her mind, though the beam also signalled her memory. The dream had been so vivid that she was even more baffled by its incomprehensibility than if it had been obscure. One thing she was certain of, she had not played a part in it; the girl in the dream was not her – she had never owned a sports car, let alone a Ferrari, and did not covet one.

The dream had taken place in a multi-storey car park in London. Gangs of men wearing navy-blue dungarees were busy removing cars; they were emptying bay after bay without saying a word. They all looked alike in their uniforms. A girl was wandering about, looking for her car. She kept asking the removal men if they had seen it. 'It's a white Ferrari', she repeated over and over again, 'you can't miss it.' The men did not reply, and carried on deftly removing cars. A famous pop star was walking about through the empty bays, looking flummoxed. The girl went up to him and asked him if he'd seen a white Ferrari. The pop star shook his head and said he didn't know what to do, it was worse than the famine in the Ethiopian

175

Desert; he felt helpless. The girl walked away and went on searching for her car. The dream ended.

Stella rebelled at the prospect of unravelling its meaning so early in the morning; the dream she felt had nothing to do with her. I t was one of those freak offshoots, captured on some pirate wave-length, to be beamed out as dross. She turned her attention to the ray of light between the curtains. At home in Guernsey a similar bright line used to blink her gently into wakefulness, ushering the promise of clear blue skies and limpid rock pools. For a few moments, to counteract the unsettling influence of the dream, she indulged the illusion of having been woken up in her mother's house by a ray of sunshine. The particles of light in fact emanated from a lamppost outside the basement room she had moved into in Bayswater. She was not very happy about living in a basement once again, but it was all she could afford. The place was airless; a dank, musty smell pervaded the atmosphere. The divan bed sagged; the loose covers on the armchairs had seen better days; the colours of their large floral design were faded and merged with the nondescript beige ground of the fabric to achieve a truly drab effect. But as Stella remembered to tell herself, every time her eyes opened on to this depressing set-up, at least she had managed to tear herself away from Oliver Carrington and his friends. Her personal situation at the Masseys' had become just too uncomfortable. What was worse, she had not shown any skill in managing it and the memory of her failure to cope continued to humiliate her. The situation, alas, had been of her own making; she only had herself to blame for it. At times she had behaved really rashly. She let Oliver see the vivacious side of her personality, allowing herself to get carried away by her enthusiasm for art and literature whilst in his company, nagged by the uneasy feeling that she was showing off in order to seduce him intellectually

176

and then she had to redress the situation by becoming aloof once again. It was all rather silly. She felt mean as well. It was obvious that Major Carrington was susceptible to that kind of seduction; his responsiveness had become an embarrassment. It would have been dishonest of her to deny that she felt attracted to him. As fate would have it, his capabilities, his smooth practicality, the ease with which he moved in all spheres, were made to impress her; they drew her to him like magnets. If she had had to devise a formula for the perfect other half, he would have been it. The greater the practical difficulties in her life became, the more irresistible the attraction grew. The temptation to surrender at times tormented her but then, looking ahead, she saw no future for the relationship. It was doomed to failure because she was not prepared to seal it by sensual encounters.

As she lay in bed, the ill-humour induced by the dream about the multi-storey car park shifted away from the frustration of its enigma to focus on another source of disquiet – a well-known one this time – evoked by the ray of light shining through the curtains: her mother's bid for a last-chance pregnancy. The thought of the poor woman's body weakened by miscarriages; her stubborn determination to try new therapies; the time, energy and money spent on treatment, it was all so upsetting. Stella pleaded with her mother to be sensible, to settle for what she had, to find other forms of creativity, but to no avail, the woman seemed bent on self-erosion. Procreation was like a drug to her; nothing could stop the addiction, and what distressed Stella was the fact that her mother got so much encouragement, so much help from so many people to confirm the habit, as though child-bearing were the most legitimate, the most exalted form of activity a human being was capable of. Meanwhile writers and artists struggled without moral support, without grants. It was a strange world.

Stella flung the bedclothes far from her. Perhaps if she started moving about, getting ready for work, her distemper would gradually be dispelled. Not that she could stop feeling compassionate towards her mother. Her mother lived in hope and that was wrong. Hope was baneful. The Greeks were right to list it among the bad things in life and to recommend it should be eschewed. She had had the good fortune of finding the works of Greek philosophers on the library shelves at Darley Hall and had derived great comfort from their writings. Strange how, with hindsight, that period in her life, fraught with fear and suspicion as it had been, appeared in retrospect as an almost happy one! For one thing, hope had not marred it (there was nothing to hope for then, whereas at present the threat of hope hovered over her emotional life like a blind enemy, much to her chagrin). Then, at Darley Hall, she had been in constant touch with the natural world and, through her horse, with the animal kingdom. Unknown to her, it had been a time of endowment. Slow-witted, she was being instructed in self-knowledge through loss; now she lived without Nature's bounties, she realized all she missed. The discovery mortified her.

To avoid self-pity and divert her thoughts from stock considerations about the inconsistencies of human nature, Stella turned on the radio. No sound issued from it. Surprised, she changed stations, to no effect. It was only when she switched wavelengths that the radio began to emit sound, in a foreign tongue. Puzzled, she walked over to the television set and turned it on. A picture appeared right away on the screen; Stella stifled a cry. Blurred and badly transmitted, it showed soldiers in camouflage suits milling around the studio, soundlessly, ghostlike. They were armed with rifles and machine-guns. The scene presented a state of confusion. Men and women in civilian

178

clothes were being ousted from the studio, protesting, or so it seemed, in a kind of silent film, for no sound came out of their moving lips. Stella switched off the television as though it were a lethal weapon. Outside, the streetlamp went out; the ray of light between the curtains vanished. A fearful speculation began to take shape in her mind. What if her dream about the men in uniform removing vehicles from the multi-storey car park had been premonitory? If she went out now to the nearest car park in Hyde Park, what would she see in the bays instead of cars?

Alarmed by apprehensions, she hastily put on the clothes which were laid out on the chair. She had been out to dinner the night before at her new employer's house and now found herself in a long skirt in oatmeal tweed with a gold thread running through it, and an ivory satin blouse (her employer's wife had complimented her on her good taste, which praise had gratified Stella's feminine vanity since she had bought the outfit for a song in a charity shop off Charing Cross Road). She slipped on the beige suede shoes she had worn the night before, but straight away took them off and put on a pair of boots, just in case. She felt disoriented, in the throes of the most inexplicable nervous discord, wondering what breach of order she would find outside. If it matched in any way the disorder that was afflicting her system, it would indeed be in the nature of a senseless dream. She grabbed her handbag; her key was in it, but there was something missing. Oh, yes, her passport! That was kept in a suitcase on top of the wardrobe. She looked at the ceiling light; it was not swaying; all the same, she felt she ought to take her passport with her. She remembered her father saying, when they spent their last holiday together in Turkey before he died, 'As soon as you feel a tremor, grab your passport and run into the garden away from tall buildings.' The feeling of panic was the same. The suitcase fell

179

on the floor and spilt its contents. On bended knees, she searched for her passport amongst newspaper cuttings, old photographs and faded envelopes. One letter in particular caught her attention. It was the one Major Carrington had sent her care of Darley Hall after that dreadful episode at Miss Beaumont's bungalow; it was written in a beautiful flowing hand. She picked up the lot and crammed it inside her handbag. The passport, she noticed, had expired.

As she ran up the area steps, an air frost, which must have occurred in the small hours, smacked her face; it penetrated her thin satin blouse. She would have run back down to fetch a coat if she had not been caught at the top of the steps in a crowd of people, all pressing forward; the surge proved too strong for her to turn round. Breathlessly she asked where they were heading for.

'To the underground station,' a man replied.

'Why?'

'To see if the trains are running.'

Normally she travelled to work by bus, but in the circumstances the underground might be safer and warmer; in any case, she could not have broken loose from the stampede, even if she tried. There was no longer any necessity for her to get into the park to check on her dream, as she had intended; her curiosity about the multi-storey car park was being satisfied gratuitously. Coming from behind. the unending rumble of tanks was heard rolling down the Bayswater Road. It was not a sound Stella relished. In fact, she had developed an aversion to it, having witnessed the persistent damage the tanks had done to the moors round Darley Hall.

The underground station was heavily guarded. Nobody knew how the soldiers had got there – they were everywhere, impersonal, nameless, inscrutable under their helmets. Londoners were invited to move along, to

180

go to work, to carry on as usual. Stella was amazed to see what a calming effect the station setting had on passengers once they got down to the familiar routine of boarding trains and alighting from them.

'Season ticket, Miss?'

'Oh, what? Oh, no, I travel by bus.'

'Get on the tube. Pay at the other end.'

Bewildered, Stella watched carriage after carriage glide past. Each time the automatic doors opened, two soldiers jumped out and stood on the platform while commuters got on, then jumped back in seconds before the doors slammed to. She had not the faintest idea what line to get on. A train stopped in front of her; she boarded it. As it rattled on through the underground, she tried to ask one of the guards how to get to Charing Cross, but the noise was so terrible she could not get them to hear. She looked up at the maps on the wall. She had got on the wrong line and had to change at Baker Street. She dreaded the thought. The oddity of her attire made her feel self-conscious. Suddenly the doors clanked open; she saw a name on the platform and rushed out just in time. She put her hands down over her knees to stop the draught blowing through the platform from ballooning her skirt; soon the weight of people pressing against her in their haste to get out enabled her to release the pressure. Although propelled forward, she felt lost. The hubbub was terrible. Passengers rushing down the stairs to get to the platform corresponding to their destinations met those who had just got off the trains headlong, and as they crossed one another on the stairs, there were hurried exchanges of garbled news.

The wildest rumours were going round, that Broadcasting House was under siege, that the Home Secretary and the Lord Chancellor had been taken hostage, that the King had abdicated in favour of his eldest son, that the

181

Commissioner of Police of the Metropolis had resigned, that the Crown jewels had been transferred under military escort from the Tower of London to the vaults of the Bank of England, that shopkeepers fearing loot and pillage by the troops had barricaded their shops and bread queues had begun all over London. As for petrol, the military had seized all service stations to refuel their vehicles.

'What about Hyde Park?' Stella shouted. 'Have people recovered their cars yet?' Her voice was submerged in the tumult. Wearily she followed the sign for the Bakerloo line. Her footsteps felt heavy. She kept looking in the direction of the exit, thinking that she ought to make a dash for it, but her will power failed her. She let Fate toss her.

The carriage she got into was even noisier and more uncomfortable than the first one she travelled in. The soldiers straddled by the doors; to steady themselves they rested the butts of their rifles on the floor between their feet; their faces remained impassive. The train stopped. Stella got out and started walking towards the exit. She thought, how ridiculous to be going to work in the outfit she had worn the night before, when she had been entertained by her employer and his wife at their house. What would his reaction be when she appeared before him wearing the same clothes?

As she emerged in the main hall, she was immediately engulfed in a multitude of passengers. At first the chaos was so overwhelming that it looked as though they were all going in different directions, but after a while it became apparent that they were in fact divided into two main streams, one being filtered out towards the exit and the other being driven back to the trains.

'Charing Cross Road,' Stella shouted at the top of her voice.

'You won't get through,' a woman said, 'all westbound traffic has been stopped.'

'But I'm going east,' Stella protested.

The woman eyed her with disdain.

'Don't get fresh with me, young lady. Anybody who goes about dressed the way you are at this time of the morning can't possibly tell east from west!'

Stella felt near to tears. She turned about and started pushing her way as hard as she could through the crowds that were coming athwart in order to join the outgoing stream.

When she got within sight of the soldiers she again shouted, 'Charing Cross Road,' and added, 'I work in Charing Cross Road.' One of the soldiers heard her and made a lane for her with his automatic rifle. She gathered the folds of her skirt together to make it less voluminous and squeezed through.

For the second time that morning she emerged out of doors. She felt immensely relieved to be out in the fresh air. She cast a quick look at the sky over the rooftops – it was blue, clear, crisp. She hurried along up Charing Cross Road, hardly daring to look around. Behind her up above, she could hear the drone of helicopters flying round and round; there must have been hundreds. For the first time that morning she felt scared. She wanted to run. Many pedestrians were running. Others stood on street corners gazing at the sky, heedless of the confusion around them. From a distance, Stella saw a queue outside the newsagents where she sometimes bought periodicals on her way to work. Level with her on the same pavement, passers-by stopped outside a television and radio shop; their eyes were glued to the screens of the sets on display in the window. The picture they were staring at was almost the same as the one Stella had seen earlier on; it showed soldiers standing guard inside the television studios. While

Stella was watching, the manager came to the front of the shop and hung a notice in the window which said 'Business as Usual'. Stella hurried on. She soon reached the Institute where she worked, but it was closed and the burglar alarm was still on. A notice had been pinned to the door – 'Due to unforeseen circumstances, the Institute will remain closed throughout the day'. Surprised, Stella looked at her wrist to find out what time it was, but in the rush of leaving home she had forgotten to put on her watch. She peered through several shop windows to see if she could spot a clock. When she succeeded she realized with a shock that it was much later than she thought. Her employer had come and gone. She was wondering what to do when she heard a familiar sound approaching fast; tanks were hurtling down Charing Cross Road. People started running down the road on both sides of the pavement to see where the tanks were going. Afraid of being knocked down, Stella cut across into St Martin's Lane, but there too tanks were careering down. A man said that he had come from the Strand and the same thing happened there; apparently all the tanks were converging on Trafalgar Square. There was a lot of activity on the river, too, according to the man's son who worked at the Savoy Hotel. Soldiers were patrolling the Thames; they had seized every barge and tug along the Embankment to stock up barrels of fuel and supplies of every description.

'It looks as though they're going to set the river on fire or blow up Parliament or something. At any rate, there isn't a Bobbie in sight. That's the trouble not having a State Police!'

'You're right,' a bystander chimed in, 'a Bobbie is not the servant of the Police authorities. He or she must rely on his or her own discretion. I know what my discretion would tell me faced with an army of tanks. Besides what duties are there left for Bobbies to discharge? The bleed-

184

ing Commandos have taken over every bleeding control. The monkeys!'

'Do you think that's why the Commissioner of the Metropolitan Police has resigned?' Stella asked innocently.

'Where did you hear that?' the second man asked, looking at Stella with amazement.

'Oh, on the tube just now.'

'It's highly likely,' the man went on. 'My daughter is in the Police, that's why I know quite a bit about it.'

Stella felt exhausted; she did not think she could listen to any more gibberish. Normally at this time of morning she would be enjoying the peace and quiet of the Institute library; it was all the more enjoyable since beyond its walls and beneath its double-glazed windows, the London traffic roared . . . .

Another sudden onrush of people made the pavement unsafe. Stella ran towards St Martin-in-the-Fields. She often went to the church in her lunch hour to listen to music recitals. The church, when she entered, was deserted. The verger stood behind the doors. Occasionally he peeped out to see what was going on in Trafalgar Square and muttered, 'Oh, dear, oh, dear!'

'Shut up', Stella said peremptorily, 'you sound just like the White Rabbit in Alice in Wonderland. This is a church, not a warren.'

The strength of her own feelings surprised her, normally she was not outspoken. The verger gave her a rueful look. 'Can you tell me why we have become so unkind to one another?' he asked. 'I thank God I was brought up in a kind world.'

'Are you referring to what is going on outside the church or to our own private parley?' Stella asked.

'Both,' the verger replied. 'Some people attribute the unkindness or should I say the belligerence . . . .'

He did not finish the sentence. The church doors flew open and a gang of coloured youths erupted followed by their attackers, who were themselves being chased by soldiers. Some of the coloured youths had received severe head wounds. The noise outside in the square was deafening. Stella shut her eyes. She slipped down from the pew where she had been resting, into a kneeling position. Often at Darley Hall, in her hour of need, she prayed. She would have done the same here but no prayer welled up; she felt arid. All the verger could say was, 'Forgive them, O Lord, for they know not what they do.'

This annoyed Stella so much that she recovered her courage and retorted: 'Oh, yes, they do!' and with that she rushed out of the church. Afraid of being knocked down by the affray which was about to break out behind her, she ran askew down the steps of the church, missed her footing and fell awkwardly, twisting her ankle. She tried to get up but could not put any weight on the injured limb. Rather than hobble about, she sat down on the steps and waited for help.

A couple of armoured vehicles pulled up sharply outside the church. A posse of Military Police jumped out of them and tore up the church steps. One of them noticed Stella and retrieved his steps.

'You hurt, Miss?'

'I think I've sprained my ankle.'

'Well, if you're not too badly injured and you can walk, I would advise you to move off.'

'That's the trouble, I can't walk.'

The MP cast his eyes down at Stella's legs.

'Hang on; I'll see what I can do.' He started running up the stairs but half-way up he collided with one of his comrades, who had just come out of the church. They began whispering to each other while looking at Stella. Then they both came down the steps.

'Is this your handbag, Miss?'

'Yes. Where did you find it?'

'Inside the church.'

'It must have fallen off my lap when I knelt down to pray.'

The two soldiers withdrew a short distance away and started whispering again. Stella began to feel flustered. She was in a lot of pain and her ankle was getting bigger by the minute. Would she be able to remove the boot if the swelling was allowed to go on?

The MPs once again made their way over to her.

'Is your surname Simmons?'

'Yes, why?'

'Are you a friend of Major Carrington?'

Stella blushed. They had opened her handbag and gone through its contents without her permission.

'Give me back my handbag,' she whispered, 'and get me to the nearest hospital, I feel faint.'

The two soldiers helped Stella to get up. A military ambulance had just pulled up outside St Martin's. The wounded youths were escorted from the church and herded inside it. Their assailants, who were being packed into the Military Police vehicles, whistled as Stella hopped across the pavement towards the ambulance. Their lusty calling turned into whoops of delight when a medical orderly hoisted her aboard and her skirt billowed. Of the two – the pain caused by the sprain or the embarrassment brought to her by the way she was dressed – she could not say which was the more acute. One thing she knew – she could not tolerate life in the raw; she could not manage it in the raw. Life would have to be refined. by desperate means if necessary, for her to possess long-term forbearance . . . .

Inside the ambulance, she hardly dared look around; some of the casualties had dreadful injuries. The soldiers who were sitting on either side of her maintained a stiff bearing. Her ankle was constantly jarred by the jolt of the vehicle; she had no idea military means of transport were so uncomfortable. At times she felt tempted to ask the guards if they knew Major Carrington, but she could not bring herself to speak to them; they had searched her handbag, they had roughly handled the injured youths . . . .

The jogging stopped. The guards jumped out. They helped Stella down. She was in agony with her ankle; the swelling had increased and the boot caused the most intolerable constriction. Outside Charing Cross Hospital, there was a pile-up of civilian ambulances which the Military Police were attempting to park out of the way either by pushing them or by getting into them. An orderly appeared with a wheelchair.

'Miss Simmons?'

'Yes . . . .'

'Hop on. Sorry! I mean let yourself down into the chair. Easy there!'

'Please, cut the boot open. I can't stand the pressure any longer. '

'I can't do that out here. It might cause more damage.'

'Where are you taking me? The Casualty Department is over there.'

'They're full up. It'll be quicker in Out-Patients.'

'Can you tell me what is going on?'

'Nobody knows exactly. Some say there's been a coup. The area round Buckingham Palace is sealed off. Here, it's business as usual. Births, deaths, you know. We're lucky.'

A sergeant was waiting in the room where Stella was wheeled in.

'Miss Simmons?'

'Yes, I am Miss Simmons.'

'Major Carrington sent me. I am to take you to him as soon as your ankle has been fixed.'

'Major Carrington!' Stella exclaimed, amazed the name cropped up again. 'Where is he?'

'I am not authorized to say.'

'I'm cold. May I have a blanket?'

The sergeant snapped his fingers at the orderly who fetched a blanket. A doctor came in with a nurse. As he walked through the door, he gave Stella a quick look and then averted his eyes.

'It is possible that when we remove the boot, the sudden shock will make you pass out. Nothing a strong cup of tea can't put right . . . .' While the doctor spoke the nurse kept eying Stella with a cold, impudent gaze.

It was dark inside the armoured truck. Stella had no idea where she was being driven. Not that she cared. The incident at the hospital had confused her. It had been a relief to pass out for a few seconds, if only to stop seeing the sarcastic expression on the nurse's face. The doctor's behaviour too had been strange. Stella blamed it all on her clothes; they were definitely wrong for that time of the morning.

'Do you think that it would possible for me to go home for a change of clothes?' she asked the sergeant who sat with her in the back.

'I'm afraid not, Miss. The Major gave me strict orders.'

She thought she'd attempt a shot in the dark.

'I thought Major Carrington was in Aldershot . . .'

The sergeant did not reply.

'Do you believe in dreams, Sergeant? I had such a strange dream last night, would you like to hear it?'

'Not particularly, Miss. Not at the moment. My mind is full of other things.'

Stella laughed light-heartedly.

'You know, Sergeant, I don't think we're going to

Aldershot.'

'We're not?'

'No, I think we're still in London. I think we're being driven round and round the West End, for some reason. The trouble is that my ankle hurts a lot. They didn't give me any pain-killers at the hospital.'

'Will you shut it, Miss! Babbling away non-stop about your clothes, your dream, your ankle. It's enough to drive anybody nuts. With the Major risking his neck on the Palace roof and the Government on the verge of collapse, all you can do is talk about yourself. I don't know how you've got the nerve! If it weren't for the Major, I'd dump you here and now. Only there's nothing I would not do for the Major.'

'Why?' Stella asked icily.

'Why? 'Cos there's nobody to measure up to the Major, not in the whole Army, not in the whole caboose. 'Cos he cares, that's why!'

'Will he move into a bigger tent?'

'Are you taking the piss, or what, Miss? I don't understand you!'

'Good! We're on a par then.'

Stella perceived an acoustic change: the sound made by the moving vehicle became muffled as in a tunnel; its motion slowed down. There was a series of bumps over insulated ramps and then the engine stopped. The sergeant handed Stella a pair of crutches.

'What did you say your name was?' she asked him before standing up.

'I didn't.'

'No, I didn't think you did.'

Wherever they had arrived, it was dark, very dark. A long distance away a spotlight cast its rays through the murk. A mass of blackened faces crowded round the armoured car: their eyes expressed nothing more than

190

cursory curiosity as they stared at Stella in silence; a lot of them looked haggard under their make-up. Stella noticed a strange thing about their uniforms. A dash of colour highlighted the left sleeve of their night-blending clothing.

The sergeant exchanged a few words with the men. An inaudible mumble as far as Stella was concerned, the men's attitudes returned a very clear message of anxiety and tension.

'Major Carrington isn't back yet,' the sergeant explained, 'but Captain Flemington is here, she'll see to you.'

Stella gripped the crutches resolutely. Her head was swimming; she faltered but managed not to pass out. The sergeant opened a lane for her through a multitude of men. Halting when she paused and moving off again as she progressed, by and by he led her to an entrance and then stood aside to let her go in. Stella found herself face to face with two armed soldiers standing guard in front of a door: the door was ajar. Through the opening Stella could see Rebecca putting on her jacket in front of a camp bed that had just been slept in; she had obviously been woken up in a hurry.

The guards pushed the door wide open. Stella, crutching as expertly as she could, entered into a kind of bunker.

'Well, what was it this time?' asked Rebecca. 'The horse or the yacht?'

'Neither,' replied Stella. 'I fell down the stepway of a church.'

'Don't tell me you were refused sanctuary, you of all people!'

Stella supported herself as far as the camp bed, dropped her crutches and handbag on it and sat down.

'Tell me, why are the soldiers wearing armbands?'

'Armbands?' queried Rebecca.

'Yes, I noticed a red ribbon on their left arms.'

191

'Oh, that! It's a symbol of solidarity. Rather touching, don't you think?'

Stella lay down on the bed. The plaster on her ankle felt very heavy. She was still wearing the blanket the orderly had thrown over her shoulders in the hospital; she pulled it over her face and closed her eyes.

21

Colonel Wallace stormed into Colonel Fraser's study. The situation was too critical for civility.

From the threshold, he shouted, 'Why don't we declare a state of siege in London? Other nations do it when their capitals are in danger.'

'It's too late, Henry,' his old friend replied.

'What kind of defeatist bosh is this? It's never too late! You're not going to let the Government be toppled by a cabal of renegades, or are you?'

'It is too late. The King himself has agreed to renounce the throne for himself and his issue.'

'Renounce the divine right of kings?' exclaimed Colonel Wallace.'No sovereign can do that!'

'You mean it would be a transgression?'

'In the eyes of God, yes. The King has been anointed.'

'In that case, if I understand the implication of what you are saying, the only honourable course open to the King is *hara-kiri*! I don't think Oliver Carrington will accept martyrdom. Carrington has a deep-seated aversion to spilling blood.'

'You mean his own, don't you? The man's a coward; he won't fight.'

'I wouldn't be too sure about that. Intelligence say that he has drilled men to a supreme degree of fitness and readiness. Their command of field skills apparently is second to none. Carrington is hugely popular with his troops. His men worship him and for a very good reason – he has their welfare at heart. As you know, he defied the Minister of Defence on their behalf. They're ready to lay down their lives if he asks them to. I think the King is right to accept to go quietly for his own sake, for his family's sake and for the nation's sake.'

'Oliver was always casting about for notoriety. He's nothing but a cheap opportunist.'

'Henry, the opportunities were there, we made them! We blundered and we bungled. Things should never have been allowed to come to such straits and you know it!'

'Those are treasonable words!'

'No, reasonable ones, Henry. The game is up.'

'Game, did you say? Since when has monarchy been a game? I'll tell you what's a game: the conspiracy of upstarts! The King must fight and we must rally round him and his family.'

'Fight? We? Under whose command and what with? You must come to your senses, Henry. The rebels are inside the Palace; they hold the King. The King himself has agreed to a deposition. Let's face it. The coup bears all the signs of careful planning and resolute leadership. The timing and organization of the entire operation take one's breath away. For sheer ingenuity it compares with the most artful exploits in military history.'

'Have you gone over to the enemy or what?' screamed Colonel Wallace.

'No, Henry,' Colonel Fraser replied calmly, 'you know as well as I do that this caper is not for us; we're fossils. What would we do in that new Model Army? Just to think of it makes me shudder. No more formality, no more barriers! Carrington talks to the men as though they were his peers.'

'The man's a traitor. He must be liquidated. What are

194

Intelligence doing about it?'

'Well, you know, they're taking the view that the strain of novelty will kill Carrington faster than an assassin. Why waste a bullet? I'm tempted to agree with them. An officer who has spent his life in tanks on the Rhine, that is not the stuff Dictators are made of, is it, even though the man has revealed himself to be a brilliant tactician?'

'Oh, I don't agree! While he fiddled away on the Rhine, his sick brain had plenty of time to elaborate schemes for self-aggrandizement.'

'His confederates haven't got the calibre either: they won't be much help to him when it comes to devising dictatorial innovations and I don't mean the rank-and-file (we all know what nitwits troopers are). I mean the commissioned officers he's roped in, the blokes from Hong Kong and Gibraltar. He's promised them all jobs.'

'But the British people won't allow it!'

'Come, come, Henry! The British people have become disenchanted with Monarchy. They've realized that the King is not prepared to make personal sacrifices in order to preserve a flawless royal image.'

'Then Parliament won't allow it!'

'The King's last constitutional act before he goes will be to dissolve Parliament. Carrington requests it.'

'The hypocritical blackguard! He breaks every rule and yet he insists on one final act of constitutional legality. He's trying to bribe the British people; he knows their love of conformity, and at the same time he has the satisfaction of manipulating the King. It is abhorrent. When I think that for years I nursed that snake in my bosom; I looked on him as my son; and the woman's no better!'

'Woman? Carrington has a large following amongst women.'

'Ay, Flemmie's daughter. Rebecca.'

'Your Rebecca? That sophisticated charmer I used to

see you with at the Club?'
   'The very same.'
   'You mean . . . .'
   'I'm afraid so.'
   'Well, well, well!'

22

'Why don't you stay here a bit longer? At least until the state of emergency is lifted? It may only last a couple of days.'

Stella gave Oliver a sidelong glance; she was beginning to feel stale for lack of fresh air.

'I need some more clothes,' she pointed out quietly.

'I can't let you go on your own,' Oliver remarked firmly. 'Rebecca will take you in her Scout car.'

'Oh, no, I can manage. I'll take a bus.'

'All bus services have been suspended for the day. You know that!' Oliver objected.

'Oh, yes, of course! I had forgotten. Well, in that case I'll take the tube.'

'Is it wise with your dodgy ankle?'

'It feels much stronger.'

Oliver shook his head.

'I can't let you go alone. I'll get Bates to take you.'

'Bates?' enquired Stella.

'Sergeant Bates. It was Bates I sent to fetch you from the hospital.'

'Oh. I never knew his name . . . a most loyal servant. I was impressed. Please, let me go on my own!'

'You are free to go. I was merely trying to point out it might be advisable not to go without an escort today of all days.'

197

Stella sulked in silence. The bunker stank; she was suffocating in its insalubrious atmosphere.

'Why did you send for me in the first place?' she asked sullenly.

'You were in danger,' Oliver replied, 'in mortal danger.'

'Well, I'm not any more. Trains are running. I'll be safe in the underground. Can't you see? I miss the library at the Institute. I need to talk to my employer. I can't breathe in this bunker. I'm tired of your endless discussions, your altercations about Northern Ireland, your wrangles over Army pay. What has all this got to do with me? And on top of everything, I have to put up with Rebecca. She represents everything I detest in a woman!'

An expression of painful surprise crept over Oliver's face.

He turned to one of his bodyguards and said, 'Take Miss Simmons to the nearest tube station.'

When Stella had picked up her suitcase, he walked over to the door with her.

'I ascribe your outburst to claustrophobia,' he said very softly. 'From down here, the library at the Institute must look like an ivory tower. Make the most of it!'

As soon as she stepped out of the bunker into the armoured car Stella heaved a sigh of relief: she had escaped! The last thing she wanted was to be seen by her landlady in the company of rebels, especially as she felt that she had been involved by accident, or was it by force? With a sprained ankle she had not had much choice. She could not help feeling cross with Oliver for having compromised her. Peace of mind, she hoped, would return when she reached the Institute.

As she made the return journey on the underground, she felt like someone coming back from the dead, the same yet not the same – encumbered by the memory of things heard and seen in the underworld, yet relieved from it. The first thing she noticed when she entered her room was the suitcase that had burst open in the middle of the floor that fateful morning, when the trouble had started. It lay where it had landed, grotesque, slightly obscene; she quickly picked it up and piled clothes into it to give it a more respectable appearance. Her eyes travelled round the dingy room. She hated everything about it. She closed the suitcase and, lifting it off the floor, walked out with it.

The prospect of travelling by tube a second time dampened her spirits. A bus ride was just what she needed, especially as the weather was dull. London had so much to offer by way of street entertainment; the red double-decker buses provided colour; they brightened up the most cheerless winter's day. But it was not to be. Buses were prohibited from leaving their depots, by order from the Committee of Public Safety, who feared reprisals against the rebel army as it staged its triumphant march through London. All motor traffic had in fact been banned from the West End. As soon as the march-past had been announced, gangs of malcontents had barricaded streets by overturning cars and erecting wire mesh banks as symbols of protest. There was not much else they could organize to oppose a leader who had armed forces to do his bidding. Tanks had made nothing of the obstacles.

As she sat on the tube, Stella could not help noticing how different things looked. To the panic of that first journey a few days ago had succeeded apathy. She read indifference, lassitude even, on passengers' faces. People kept very quiet. Remembering the frenzied rumours which flew around, on the first morning, out of one train into another, from station to station, there prevailed an atmosphere of unconcern. Stella did not know whether to rejoice over it or to deplore it. Deep in her heart she could not help feeling vindictive towards Oliver for having abducted her; therefore, regrettably, she was pleased to see that people did not seem to care.

When she arrived at the Institute she went straight upstairs to the library. She was so happy to be back! The library was empty except for one reader at the far end of the room, by one of the windows overlooking Charing Cross Road. He peered over the top of his spectacles when he saw Stella coming in and then resumed reading. Stella put away her suitcase behind her desk. She intended to go and see the Director in his office to ask if she could stay at the Institute till the end of the state of emergency. As she was about to leave the library, she heard a cough coming from behind one of the partitions of book shelves. Peering round the corner, she saw her employer concealed in the shadows of a recess; he put a finger up to his lips when he saw Stella.

'Shoosh!' he whispered, casting a glance in the direction of the reader by the window. He then grabbed Stella by the arm and gently pushed her into an even more remote corner of the library. 'Stella. my dear child, we've been worried stiff about you! You look terrible! You're limping! Where have you been? Have those sharpshooters been bullying you?'

He was talking in whispers. His tousled grey hair gave him an unfamiliar look; he was normally dapper.

'Just the person I wanted to see. I'll be brief. These walls have ears.' As he spoke, he kept looking round the corner at the old man who was reading by the window. 'I know I can count on your discretion. I mean, you are one of us.'

'Oh, I am a book lover, if nothing else, Mr Devereux!'

'That's not quite what I meant; your love of books is unquestionable. What I meant was, a loyal subject. We, loyalists, have got to stick together. The future of democracy is in jeopardy. The fabric of our social order is under threat; we can't let those gunmen shoot it to tatters, can we? As you know, this Institute has connections abroad, in Sweden, in Denmark and the Low Countries and in the Commonwealth.'

'But I thought this Institute was strictly non-political!' Stella objected tearfully.

'Political? You call that *charivari* political?' asked Mr Devereux raising his voice. Almost immediately he realized that he had allowed his feelings to run away with him; he dropped his voice down the register a tone or two and began whispering again. 'Don't delude yourself, Stella. It has nothing to do with politics, it has to do with . . . ,' Mr Devereux leant over closer to Stella's face, and spat out the word 'tyranny'.

'We fight military dictatorships abroad, don't we? It's not cricket, is it?'

At times Mr Devereux's manner of speech, caring and intimate, reminded Stella of the way her father used to speak to her when they had their 'heart-to-heart' talks, to elucidate points of conduct at home or misdemeanours at school, when with good humour and patience he would come down to her level. She almost felt guilty Mr Devereux's confidentiality did not inspire her with gratitude.

'You mean "Fair is Foul"?' she asked wide-eyed.

'I knew you would understand. Your culture warranted it. We loyalists must unite; we must organize clandestine meetings, resist by every possible means, bring the King back. It may take years, decades, half a century, who knows? You understand, don't you, Stella? It'll mean holding out.'

'Yes, I understand.'

'Not a very cheerful prospect, but we always win in the end, don't we? We always manage to bring things back to normal. That's what we've got to remember.'

Stella shook her head.

'I knew I could count on you.'

They heard a sudden clatter. The old man had got up and pulled back his chair. Mr Devereux motioned Stella forward with authoritative hand gestures. The old man handed Stella the books he had borrowed.

'Well,' he said, 'I had better run along before the fireworks start. I am past that sort of amusement. Who would have thought it would come to this? Mind you . . . .'

A horrified look came over Stella's face.

'Never mind,' said the old man, getting the message, 'some other time.'

When he had gone, Mr Devereux emerged from behind the partition. He took Stella by the arm and steered her towards a table under one of the windows. He offered her a chair and sat down opposite.

'As I was saying when we were interrupted, I knew I could count on you.'

Stella took a deep breath and got up.

'Mr Devereux, I am afraid it is time for my appointment at the hospital. I need a different type of support for my ankle.'

'Good, Good,' Mr Devereux replied, scanning Stella's face. 'Get that ankle right. We need people like you. Are you leaving your suitcase here?'

'No, I had better take it with me in case they have to keep me in.'

'That's a very sensible idea considering the order of the day: anything might happen.'

Stella negotiated the Institute stairs as fast as she could, handicapped as she was both by her injured ankle and the suitcase. By leaving the Institute she was gaining freedom; no time should be lost in embracing it. The ivory tower

202

mentioned by Oliver in a fit of pique was not the library at the Institute. It was her own mind; there she was free to dwell, a liege to no one.

She was walking better, she thought. Her steps gravitated towards St Martin-in-the-Fields, a place she had a predilection for, why she could not fathom. Perhaps its bucolic name appealed to her; or then the contrast between the pastoral picture it conjured in her imagination and the densely built-up area that had swallowed up the rustic setting over the centuries? Whatever the reason, that area of London evoked an Arcadian past she was susceptible to.

She needed to indulge herself emotionally. The last few days inside the bunker had been purgatory. She had known utter spiritual deprivation, except for a few highly-charged moments when she had befriended a young trooper who wrote songs.

She was relieved to see that the church was empty. Thinking about it, it was not surprising. Who would have elected it as a resort when a spectacular was about to take place outside? For her it provided an ideal retreat. She could sit and meditate for a while and she could too, if she felt like it, stand outside and watch the march past. She knew, for having overheard Oliver and his acolytes plan the whole thing in its minutest details, what route the troops on parade would follow. Already the buildings round Trafalgar Square were teeming with heavily armed security guards. Marksmen were posted on all the roofs. Oliver had ordered an incredible number of precautionary measures to avoid turmoil.

What a strange man he was! First and foremost a soldier. When she had woken up in the bunker that first day (or was it night?), her face still covered up, Oliver was speaking to the men. His voice quivered with solicitude as he enquired about their welfare, urging them to rest. He congratulated each one of them on the speed and precision with which they had dispatched their duties and thanked them very warmly. His account of the seizure of the King was devoid of any trace of animosity, or any feeling of personal triumph. When the troops asked him if the King was going to speak to the nation, he replied that he had advised the monarch against it. The King had suffered enough loss of prestige at the hands of the media to humiliate himself publicly one last time; he was to go with dignity. When Rebecca begged him to get some sleep, he replied, 'The King is not sleeping. Why should I?'

Stella had to admit that she had never understood him. He was unlike anybody she had ever known, either in real life or in fiction. Grudgingly she credited Rebecca with an insight into Oliver's character that she herself had never possessed. Rebecca had understood how to make Oliver take notice of her: she had ingratiated herself by espousing his military ideal.

At that stage in her meditation, Stella was choked by a terrible sense of inadequacy. At one time, in Aldershot, at the Masseys', she and Oliver had grown very close to each other. True, he had kept her in the dark about his military ambitions, but, she asked herself, would it have made any difference to their relationship, such as it was, if he had taken her into his confidence? She would still have remained the same reserved person with her inhibitions, her fundamental intellectuality, her distaste for practical life. She would have been no good for him.

Today, for instance, what help would she be to him when his self-appointed mandate awaited the verdict of public opinion? The King had been deposed; already the King's Flight had been given its last assignment – to fly Him and His family to Australia, where they would remain in exile for the rest of their lives (their livestock to

204

follow immediately after). After this dramatic develop-
ment, who could say what kind of reception Oliver would
get from bewildered citizens, when he appeared for the
first time at the head of his troops, and what role could
she, a librarian, have played in the making of history, had
she remained at his side? The Army Press had printed
thousands of leaflets explaining the structure of the provisional government which Oliver had already
announced over the air. It was to take the form of a
Decemvirate, comprising seven soldiers (one of whom was
a woman Captain Rebecca Flemington, Foreign Relations) and three civilians, the Administrator of Justice, the
Administrator of Finance and the Curator of the Environment. According to some of the officers in the bunker, the
creation of the post of Administrator of Justice was bound
to cause an uproar since there had never been a Minister
of Justice in the cabinet of His Majesty's Government
under the old regime. Stella had no particular thoughts
on the matter and felt at a loss to express an opinion,
either for or against. Tongue-tied and inarticulate when it
came to current affairs, she conceded another advantage
to Rebecca, who, even if she could not put forward any
original ideas, at least acquainted herself daily with
Oliver's views on all major issues and could join in.

Only the works of poets, of philosophers and great
novelists had ever had the power to unloose her tongue.
She grew loquacious, lyrical even, over them in a way few
people imagined because it belied her taciturn manner.
Looking back, she was glad she had spoken freely to
Oliver on literary subjects. She had made no secret about
her propensity for certain authors, always hoping for a
sign from him to say he shared her interest, but up to the
day of the coup, he had never shown any enthusiasm for
literature. She suspected him of never having read a
classic. On the night of the coup, the realization that he

205

was through and through a military man brought a slant on this void. Creative writing did arouse Oliver, but only when it appealed to his emotions as a soldier! Her amazement when she discovered this only served to give her further proof of her lack of percipience in his respect.

There was a young trooper in one of Oliver's units who wrote songs. He played his own tunes on the recorder; the instrument suited his melancholy personality. After the coup, when the unit this wistful young man belonged to had been relieved from its turn of duties outside the Palace, Stella chanced to hear the young trooper soothing away his exhaustion on the recorder. From time to time he would put the recorder down and hum a few mournful words. Then he would pick up the recorder again and express the same feeling of sadness up and down a scale of wailing sounds. The pathos of his performance had gone straight to her heart. She told the young man how moved she had been by the little she'd heard. The ballad, he said, was of his own composition; he would be pleased to sing it to her in its entirety, including a few bars here and there on the recorder to enhance the effect. Oliver was standing close by when the recitation started; he immediately came over to the space on the crowded floor where the young man had propped himself up.

'I have called this song "The Old Battleship", I wrote it for my mates.

> "The Battleship England is sinking,
> Off the Isle of Sheppey
> Scuttled by rats from tower to galley,
> The good old battleship England.
> How she lurches! How she rolls!
> Her power ebbs away,
> With none to see and none to cry,
> Off the Isle of Sheppey.

206

O Stranger, were you to ask me why,
Forsaken by all her ranks
She lists to starboard on mud banks,
I'd let my heart tell thee:
She who once beamed liberty
On the spillways of the sea,
Has lost all hands save a stalwart few,
Amongst whom I counted thee."

Oliver was visibly affected by the song.

'Why Sheppey?' he asked, while adjusting the trooper's red ribbon which had slipped down his arm.

'That's where I come from, Sir. The beach is covered with old wrecks.'

He then straightened up and looking at the young man said impromptu,

" 'O soldier, were you to ask me why
She was salvaged by a stalwart few,
I'd let my heart tell thee:
They raised a pennant and an army
Amongst whose ranks I counted thee . . . .' "

Stella knew that she had come to the end of her meditation; she could bear no more pain. She also knew that there was no hurt beyond the acceptance of truth. She felt ready to leave the shelter of the church. She would go outside and watch the armoured motorcade. When it was all over, she would wend her way back to her basement room in Bayswater. She promised herself that she would not allow its dinginess to depress her too much.

23

Below the church pedestrians had begun to assemble on the pavement. Stella knew, having overheard Oliver and the Army Council discuss the arrangements, that the armoured motorcade would start in Hyde Park. Oliver, who was still keyed up, insisted on maintaining a state of full-scale alert; he was reluctant to relax discipline so early on; he wanted the men kept at the peak of readiness. He would bivouac in Hyde Park with the pick of his troops (after having lived underground in nuclear shelters, the fresh air would do them all the world of good), review his own regiment of tanks after Reveille the next day; on the way out call a brief halt outside Buckingham Palace to watch the Royal Standard being lowered for the last time and the banner of St George raised in its place, then move off to collect the armoured vehicles massed outside Wellington Barracks before proceeding down The Mall. Stella remembered the order in which the armoured motorcade was to be displayed had caused most of the arguments between Oliver and his officers. They wanted him to go first in his tank and he wanted the troopers to be in front. She was curious to see who had won and kept her eyes peeled.

Rebecca came first! Stella closed her eyes. She waited a few seconds before opening them again, just long enough not to have to see Rebecca's jubilant face. Rebecca was chauffeur-driven. She sat in the back of her Scout car; two soldiers carrying bazookas walked ahead of the car and two more, constantly challenging, moved alongside it. Next came the soldiers on foot in camouflage suits, the red ribbons Stella had noticed on the night of the coup still tied round their left arms. Then Oliver appeared in his tank, flying his personal emblem, the banner of St George. He was standing up in the hatch, hatless; a dozen men carrying arms sat round him on top of his vehicle in rather relaxed positions. Behind his tank, an endless vista of armoured vehicles, four abreast, stretched as far as the eye could see.

In front of Oliver's tank, Stella saw a strange-looking man. He wore a faded red beret; an accordion was slung across his shoulder; he had a puppy at heel on a short lead, a West Highland terrier. Someone on the pavement below shouted 'Look at the little dog!'

'Isn't it sweet!' exclaimed another bystander. 'It must be their mascot!'

So far none of the spectators who were standing close by had expressed any enthusiasm for the impressive display of military might which was coming their way. At the sight of the little dog their indifference melted. They started clapping, quietly at first, then, as the puppy's owner responded by performing several pirouettes and playing a few imaginary chords on the accordion, the applause increased. People who lined the route began to run alongside the armoured motorcade to keep level with the terrier and its entertaining handler. Part of Oliver's bodyguard jumped off his tank to block the headlong rush, but still, as the motorcade advanced and more people set eyes on the dog, the plaudits went on, picked up from one section of the crowd by another in steady relays.

The access to Trafalgar Square was now jammed on all sides by tanks. From where she stood Stella could watch the movement of troops taking up their allotted positions in front of the National Gallery. The inane cheering and clapping of the crowd ceased as the dog disappeared. A hush settled over the place; only the sounds of isolated military commands, fraught with subdued emotion, snapped across the Square.

Rebecca got out of her car. She took up her position on the bottom step of the left-hand stairway of the Gallery. She looked better in uniform than she did in those baggy safari suits of hers; she had nice legs . . . pity she smiled so complacently, but then no doubt her smugness would stand her in good stead; as Foreign Emissary she would prove a valuable asset . . . .

She greeted Oliver at the bottom of the stairs. Stella could not see their faces as they climbed together to the top. Under the portico a group of soldiers were waiting; they shook hands with Oliver and then they embraced one another while Rebecca stood aside. The silence in the Square was oppressive. The troops were massed shoulder to shoulder. A young trooper ran up the stairs carrying the banner of St George as though it were a flame and held it behind Oliver. A tremendous roar went up, shattering the restraint of previous moments.

Stella sensed a change of mood. Puzzled Londoners, who had stood wavering on the outskirts of the Square, started moving in. Something incredible was happening at the heart of their City, in their Square – perhaps they ought to take a closer look? After all, there were no food shortages; no disruptions of train services; fuel was plentiful. Yet theirs was a city without a King, without a police; the Government had fled, some to Scotland, some abroad . . . . From the sky thousands of multi-coloured leaflets were being dropped by helicopter over the Square. They fluttered in the air, ascending and descending in riveting spirals. mingling with flocks of pigeons on the wing before touching down. A man on the pavement below the church picked up a leaflet.

He waited for the last helicopter to circle away then looking up at Stella he called out to her, 'King John, he was mad, wasn't he? Yet he gave us Magna Carta, didn't he? And this King, what has he done for us? What has he given us?'

Stella nodded to signify her assent. She was terrified the man would come and join her if she took issue with him, but he turned away again towards the Square when he finished speaking. Oliver had put his hands up to still the clamour that had gone up from the crowd. He was now standing by himself under the portico right in front of the balustrade. He waited for the troops to stop fidgeting. Stella knew he had promised them a speech; he was obviously about to deliver it.

'Today,' he began, through a loud-hailer, 'today does not mark the dawn of a new era. Today marks the birthday of a new man, your birthday, and yours, and yours,' (he was pointing in the direction of the crowd). 'Today you are born anew, with new eyes, with a new heart and a new mind. New eyes to enable you to look at reality; a new heart to tackle reality and a new mind to take stock of reality. The hearts and minds you had before were never properly stimulated and they perished from loss of use.

'Every man and woman who is born today is born to an inheritance and that inheritance is THIS land. You are all co-heirs to this great land of ours and as co-heirs, you must claim your inheritance, your birthright, and not only must you lay claim to it, but you must also honour it. You must redeem it, that is you must regain possession of it by paying a price! What price will you pay for this great land of yours, you who have been given so much, so extravagantly by spendthrift rulers, without ever being

211

told you had an obligation? Their largesse bought you out, and now you must buy yourselves in – through toil, through hard work. When you have paid the price and you have re-possessed the land, you will become share-holders in the largest concern of them all, our country. Together, soldiers and civilians side by side, we shall till the land; we shall mine the coal; we shall drill the oil. But do not think it will all be plain sailing. A lot of it – most of it – will be fighting a rearguard action against neglect, pollution and abuse through greed. Unpatriotic parasites, unwilling to assist in this arduous enterprise, will be prosecuted without respite.

'I thank you all for the steadfastness with which you have supported me in our mutual quest for a new identity, more in keeping with the times. May the future hold true its promise of fulfilment to all of you, new men, till our task is completed and beyond.'

There was a minute of silence, then a voice down in the Square shouted:

'Three cheers for the Major! Hip hip!'

'Hurrah!'

'Hip, hip!'

'Hurrah!'

'Hip, hip!'

'Hurrah!'

The troops packed in the Square broke their ranks. They clambered up on the lions and the fountains, took off their hats and waved them frantically chanting 'Carr-ington!, Carrington!' The tankmen brought out their tools. They proceeded to bang them against the tops of their armoured vehicles with unflagging energy to accom-pany their comrades' chorus. Small groups of civilians stood bewildered on the edge of the Square, not knowing what to do. One of the soldiers spotted a pretty girl and offering her his hand helped her to climb on the lion where he perched. Others followed his example.

The man who had brought up Magna Carta turned his head towards the church and seeing Stella was still there shouted, 'Pity he isn't an Admiral of the Fleet!'

Stella pretended she had not heard.

'That Major Carrington! It would have gone down better. Still, I suppose we've got to give it a try. It's only fair, isn't it?'

Stella shook her head. Disappointed the man turned away and approached another civilian in the street below.

The racket in the Square kept getting worse. Stella felt that the troops were becoming delirious and she feared mass hysteria would ensue; already passion was mounting on both sides.

Oliver came back to the balustrade of the portico. He waved to the crowds that were gathered directly in front of the National Gallery, then he pivoted to acknowledge the cheers of the people on the left-hand side of the Square. He was now looking in the direction of St Martin-in-the-Fields. All of a sudden he stopped waving. Stella saw him staring at her across the Square over a multitude of heads. Slowly she raised her hand and waved to him. Tears were running down her face. She did not know whether they were tears of joy or tears of contrition, or the tears one sheds on parting from loved ones, and he, remembering that other time many months ago when she had come down the front steps of Darley Hall, a diminutive figure clad in blue, dwarfed by the size of the house, waved back (this time she was dressed in white). His hand hung limply in the air, without motivation; he did not know why he was waving, to acknowledge what? Then his attention was restored; he turned away from the church and faced the crowds on the right hand side of the Square to acknowledge their cheers.

A shot rang out. Stella reeled, clutching her throat. She

213

tried not to fall. Her cries for help were drowned in a vortex of yells. She was caught in its spin. It revolved faster and faster, echoed louder and louder. When it burst, she slumped to the ground.

EPILOGUE

Rebecca's driver was perusing an issue of the *Army Gazette* when his mother called him.

'Edwin . . . .'

'Yes, Mother?'

'I wish you'd throw away some of those old newspapers; they collect the dust.'

'What old newspapers?'

'All those back numbers of the *Army Gazette*.'

'Mother! They're archives, historical documents; they recount the daily events of the Revolution. In fifty years' time, they'll be worth a fortune.'

'Couldn't you keep just a few?'

'Such as?'

'Oh, I don't know! The most memorable ones, I suppose, the ones that illustrate whatever it was that made Carrington such a special person in your eyes.'

'Mother! They're all memorabilia! Each one of them contains a gem! Take this one for instance. A laconic bulletin appeared in it which speaks volumes for Carrington's – what shall I call it? Tact? Graciousness? – It concerns Colonel Wallace, who was like a father to him. Anyone not in the know would miss the point entirely.'

'Come on, then! I know I'm ignorant.'

'A few days after the provisional government was set up, the old boy committed suicide. To keep the Colonel's memory unblemished Carrington had this bulletin published: "Colonel Henry Archibald Wallace was found

215

dead at his house yesterday. It is widely believed in official circles he shot himself accidentally while cleaning his gun" It was Carrington's way of paying tribute to an old friend who had become an enemy.'

Edwin's mother mulled over her son's disclosure for a while. 'Edwin . . . .'

'Yes, Mother?'

'Where do you think Carrington is now?'

Rebecca's driver raised his eyebrows. He hesitated before answering. His mother asked the same question nearly every day; she was convinced he kept a secret from her. His patience was beginning to wear thin.

'I don't know . . . . Some reports say he has been sighted in the United States near a launching site.'

'What do you think?'

'It's possible. He always was interested in space travel.'

'A lovely way to go?'

'Ay, to the gods in Olympus! He was too shrewd to consider deification on Earth. Other reports say he has been spotted in South America.'

'And the Star of Bethlehem?'

Edwin grinned. He loved his mother's nickname for Stella, whom he had met briefly in the bunker. 'Oh, she went with him all right! Carrington's broad shoulders proved irresistible in the end. After the attempt on her life, her nerves were badly frayed. As for Carrington, well, he had carried heavier burdens than Stella.'

'What do you think then?'

'It's difficult to say. I'd plumb for South America. My own feeling is that's where he is.'

'That's interesting. Couldn't you have said so before?'

A distant look came into the driver's eyes as he gazed inwards into his store of memories.

'I remember him saying that if he came out of the Revolution alive, he'd spend the rest of his life whale-

216

watching in Patagonia.'
　'Why Patagonia?'
　'That's where the largest whales are found.'

FINIS

POST-SCRIPTUM

In March 1649, Cromwell warned the Council of State of the threat presented by the propaganda activities in the Army of the Levellers, a radical sect with bold conceptions of Liberty and Property. 'You have no other way to deal with these men but to break them . . . If you do not break them, they will break you.'

In May 1649, Cromwell and General Sir Thomas Fairfax defeated the most dangerous Leveller-led mutiny at Burford, Oxfordshire. Many of the Levellers' ideas were driven underground as the revolution took a more conservative turn in the hands of men of property. In my book, I have attempted very fictitiously, as a lay person, to pick up the threads of some of the radical ideas of the Leveller element in the army.

It is my belief that those ideas could not die because they expressed a trait of the national character ingrained and irrepressible, always ready to spring up.